Death and Mary Dazill

MARY FITT

With an introduction by Curtis Evans

 Moonstone Press

This edition published in 2022 by Moonstone Press
www.moonstonepress.co.uk

Introduction © 2022 Curtis Evans

Originally published in 1941 by Michael Joseph Ltd

Death and Mary Dazill © the Estate of Kathleen Freeman, writing as Mary Fitt

The right of Kathleen Freeman to be identified as author of this work has been
asserted in accordance with the Copyright, Designs and Patents Act 1988

ISBN 978-1-899000-50-0
eISBN 978-1-899000-51-7

A CIP catalogue record for this book is available from the British Library

Text designed and typeset by Tetragon, London
Cover illustration by Jason Anscomb
Printed and bound by CPI Group (UK) Ltd, Croydon, CRO 4YY

Contents

INTRODUCTION

Fitting into the Past:
Mary Fitt's Death and Mary Dazill
(1941)

In 1941, when classical scholar Kathleen Freeman published her
tenth 'Mary Fitt' detective novel in five years, *Death and Mary
Dazill* (*Aftermath of Murder* in the United States), she decidedly
broke the mould of the traditional body-in-the-library, butler-did-it
country-house mystery that has become inseparable from people's
conceptions of British crime writing from that era. True, the scene
of the crimes (if crimes they are) is set at a country house—but
one with a marked difference. There is mystery, yes, and a fitting,
though long delayed, resolution to it, but the author lays particularly powerful emphasis on the psychology of it all: how a conflict of
repressed but withal roiling passions among individuals can lead to
life-altering—and -ending—tragedy. Additionally, the novel is set
in the Victorian era, making it one of the early notable expressions
in the genre of the Victorian period mystery since popularised by
Peter Lovesey and other modern crime writers.

In a 1955 interview about her crime writing, Mary Fitt (as
I shall call her henceforward), bluntly admitted that, having written

several well-reviewed but 'only moderately successful' non-genre novels, 'I really started writing detective stories because they always seem to sell, and I do so like to have an audience! What's the good of posthumous fame? I want to be there to enjoy it!' However, Fitt did not commit crime writing solely for the money, for she believed detective fiction offered her a legitimate forum for literary expression, just like the mainstream novel. One day in the mid-Thirties she had 'noticed... that almost everyone whom I liked and respected, my colleagues, my friends, my doctor, my lawyer, all [of them] read whodunits. So I thought why shouldn't I put what I have to say into that form?'

After having published nine mystery novels, the five most recent of which featured the dogged individual who would become her longtime series sleuth, Superintendent Mallett, Mary Fitt decided that she wanted to stretch the boundaries of the traditional form—as she had in her astounding debut mystery, *Three Sisters Flew Home*—in order to accommodate the things she wanted still to say. With *Death and Mary Dazill* she succeeded, in my view, in producing her best mystery since her first, a compelling story of crime and consequences that has the literary values of a mainstream novel.

Do not take my word for it, however: Mary Fitt's contemporaries thought so too. In the United States, a fascinating character named Bob Patterson, aka 'Freddy Francisco', the popular San Francisco society columnist, writing under the nom de plume 'Cholly San Francisco' gave *Mary Dazill* a nice boost indeed when he observed that it was 'far and away one of the top-notch mystery stories in a long, long time'; while multifaceted Wisconsin writer and reviewer August Derleth, whose work included both crime and horror fiction, proclaimed the novel one of the best mysteries of the year. In the United Kingdom, 'the Book Taster' in the *Liverpool Daily Post* lauded *Mary Dazill* at greater length:

> Mary Fitt's new story 'Death and Mary Dazill'... may, I suppose, be called a thriller, and it does thrill. Miss Fitt creates an atmosphere which is disturbing: her power in this respect reminds of Mrs. Belloc Lowndes [author of the crime-thriller classic *The Lodger* and other works]. Mary Dazill is a beautiful, rather mysterious girl, almost a wraith one would call her... she produces a tremendous and tragic disturbance in the house she enters a sort of governess. The nature of the disturbance I must leave the reader to discover. Miss Fitt tells her story with remarkable skill and... she writes with distinction.

Seven years after its original publication, crime writer and critic Julian Symons, in reviewing a Penguin paperback reprint of the novel in the *Manchester Evening News*, revealed that he had not yet escaped the spell of *Mary Dazill*. He reflected on the eerie and bewitching quality of the tale as follows:

> Mary Fitt has something of [M. P.] Shiel's appetite for old houses and churchyards, and 'Death and Mary Dazill'... seems to me the best of her stories.
>
> It tells of the strange doom brought on a peaceful Victorian household through the coming of Mary Dazill as companion to the two beautiful daughters of the house, Lindy and Arran.
>
> The book holds the attention of a novel, and Miss Fitt cleverly increases suspense and heightens the period atmosphere by recounting the story through the eyes of a narrator living in the present day, who tells it as unsolved mystery of the past.

As the reviews above have outlined, *Death and Mary Dazill* tells
the doomful tale of Miss Mary Dazill, a beautiful young woman
who arrives one day at Chetwode Lodge in the village of Long
Marley to act as a sort of private tutor to Lindisfarne and Arran,
the two lovely but naïve teenage daughters of the widowed Ralph
de Boulter, lately returned to England from Burma, where he
had lived with his late first wife for many years. The elder of the
two daughters, Lindy, is on the verge of engagement with John
Despenser, the son of a neighbouring family who is up at Oxford
with the girls' brother, Leonard.

Death and Mary Dazill, which has something of the quality of an
M. R. James ghost story (though the hauntings are all too human),
unfolds as a tale primarily told, in the then present day, by Mrs.
Barratt, wife of the vicar of Long Marley, she being the daughter of
a woman who was an intimate participant in the events at Chetwode
Lodge of long ago. Series sleuth Superintendent Mallett, along with
a pair of supporting characters, Doctors Fitzbrown and Jones (the
former still hyper-imaginative and the latter quite the opposite),
are told the story at the cosy vicarage at Long Marley, beginning
at tea on a drear November day after they, having come over from
Chode to attend the funeral of the local police sergeant, espy a pair
of elderly women laying a great wreath of hothouse flowers—arum
lilies, scarlet amaryllis, gardenias—at a marble memorial column.
These ladies, they learn, are the aged Misses de Boulter...

Death and Mary Dazill aired as a six-part BBC radio adaptation
in 1949, nine years after the appearance of the book. Like a character in a Freeman Wills Crofts novel, Mary Fitt, who had been
travelling in Italy, returned by bus and train to Paris, catching a
plane to London and landing there at three in the afternoon, making
it just in time to receive guests, including Lady Cynthia Asquith

and Angela Thirkell, at a cocktail party given in Kensington to celebrate the broadcast. 'I was determined to get back in time for the party,' she announced. Years later she named *Death and Mary Dazill* as her own favourite among her mysteries. (A few years later Lady Cynthia would include the Mary Fitt ghost stories 'The Amethyst Cross' and 'The Doctor' in her celebrated *Second* and *Third Ghost Book* anthologies.)

Certainly, in my own case the novel is a leading candidate for the title of 'favourite Fitt'. When originally reading it some two decades ago, I was struck by how in many ways it prefigures Shelley Smith's classic Victorian mystery *An Afternoon to Kill* (1953), which is similarly told retrospectively. There is also a resemblance to Julian Symons's own melancholy essay on fatal family dysfunction in the Victorian era, *The Blackheath Poisonings* (1978). Now *Death and Mary Dazill* has returned from crime fiction's grave, as it were, to take its rightful place in this eminently ghastly company.

ABOUT THE AUTHOR

One of the prominent authors of the classical detective fiction of the Golden Age and afterwards was herself a classicist: Kathleen Freeman, a British lecturer in Greek at the University College of South Wales and Monmouthshire, Cardiff (now Cardiff University) between 1919 and 1946. Primarily under the pseudonym Mary Fitt, Freeman published twenty-nine crime novels between 1936 and 1960, the last of them posthumously. Eighteen of these novels are chronicles of the criminal investigations of her series sleuth, Superintendent Mallett of Scotland Yard, while the remaining eleven of them, nine of them published under the pseudonym Mary Fitt and one apiece published under the respective names of Stuart Mary Wick and Kathleen Freeman, are stand-alone mysteries, some of which are notable precursors of the modern psychological crime novel. There is also a single collection of Superintendent Mallett 'cat mystery' short stories, *The Man Who Shot Birds*.

From the publication of her lauded debut detective novel, *Three Sisters Flew Home*, Mary Fitt – like Gladys Mitchell, an author with whom in England she for many years shared the distinguished publisher Michael Joseph – was deemed a crime writer for 'connoisseurs'. Within a few years, Fitt's first English publisher, Ivor Nicholson & Watson, proudly dubbed her devoted following a 'literary cult'. In what was an unusual action for the time, Nicholson & Watson placed on the dust jacket of their edition of Fitt's *Death at Dancing Stones* (1939) accolades from such distinguished, mystery-writing Fitt fans as Margery Allingham ('A fine detective story and a most ingenious puzzle'), Freeman Wills Crofts ('I should like to offer her my congratulations') and J. J. Connington ('This is the best book by Miss Mary Fitt I have yet read').

If not a crowned 'queen of crime' like Allingham, Agatha Christie, Dorothy L. Sayers and Ngaio Marsh, Kathleen Freeman in her Mary Fitt guise was, shall we say, a priestess of peccadillos. In 1950 Freeman was elected to the prestigious Detection Club, a year after her crime-writing cover was blown in the gossip column 'The Londoner's Diary' in the *Evening Standard*. Over the ensuing decade several of the older Mary Fitt mysteries were reprinted in paperback by Penguin and other publishers, while new ones continued to appear, to a chorus of praise from such keen critics of the crime-fiction genre as Edmund Crispin, Anthony Berkeley Cox (who wrote as, among others, Francis Iles) and Maurice Richardson. 'It is easy to run out of superlatives in writing of Mary Fitt,' declared the magazine *Queen*, 'who is without doubt among the first of our literary criminographers.'

Admittedly, Freeman enjoyed less success as a crime writer in the United States, where only ten of her twenty-nine mystery novels were published during her lifetime. However, one of Fitt's warmest boosters was the *New York Times*'s Anthony Boucher, for two decades the perceptive dean of American crime-fiction reviewers. In 1962, three years after Fitt's death, Boucher selected the author's 1950 novel *Pity for Pamela* for inclusion in the 'Collier Mystery Classics' series. In his introduction to the novel, Boucher lauded Fitt as an early and important exponent of psychological suspense in crime fiction.

Despite all the acclaim which the Mary Fitt mysteries formerly enjoyed, after Freeman's untimely death from congestive heart failure in 1959 at the age of sixty-one, the books, with very few exceptions – *Miʒmaʒe* (Penguin, 1961), *Pity for Pamela* (Collier, 1962), *Death and the Pleasant Voices* (Dover, 1984) – fell almost entirely out of print. Therefore, this latest series of sparkling reissues from Moonstone is a welcome event indeed for lovers of vintage British mystery, of which Kathleen Freeman surely is one of the most beguiling practitioners.

*

A native Midlander, Kathleen Freeman was born at the parish of Yardley near Birmingham on 22 June 1897. The only child of Charles Henry Freeman and his wife Catherine Mawdesley, Kathleen grew up and would spend most of her adult life in Cardiff, where she moved with her parents not long after the turn of the century. Her father worked as a brewer's traveller, an occupation he had assumed possibly on account of an imperative need to support his mother and two unmarried sisters after the death of his own father, a schoolmaster and clergyman without a living who had passed away at the age of fifty-seven. This was in 1885, a dozen years before Kathleen was born, but presumably the elder Charles Freeman bequeathed a love of learning to his family, including his yet-unborn granddaughter. Catherine Mawdesley's father was James Mawdesley, of the English seaside resort town of Southport, not far from Liverpool. James had inherited his father's 'spacious and handsome silk mercer's and general draper's establishment', impressively gaslit and 'in no degree inferior, as to amplitude, variety and elegance of stock, to any similar establishment in the metropolis or inland towns' (in the words of an 1852 guide to Southport), yet he died at the age of thirty-five, leaving behind a widow and three young daughters.

As a teenager, Kathleen Freeman was educated at Cardiff High School, which, recalling the 1930s, the late memoirist Ron Warburton remembered as 'a large attractive building with a large schoolyard in front, which had a boundary wall between it and the pavement'. The girls attended classes on the ground floor, while the boys marched up to the first (respectively, the first and second floors in American terminology). 'The first-floor windows were frosted so that the boys could not look down at the girls in the school playground,' Warburton wryly recalled. During the years of the Great War, Freeman, who was apparently an autodidact in ancient Greek (a subject unavailable at Cardiff High School, although the boys learned Latin), attended the co-educational, 'red-brick' University College of South Wales and Monmouthshire, founded three decades earlier in 1883, whence she graduated with a BA in Classics in 1918. The next year saw both her mother's untimely passing at the age of fifty-two and her own appointment as a lecturer in Greek at her alma mater. In 1922, she received her MA; a Doctor of Letters belatedly followed eighteen years later, in recognition of her scholarly articles and 1926 book *The Work and Life of Solon*, about the ancient Athenian statesman. Between 1919 and 1926 Freeman was a junior colleague at University College of her former teacher Gilbert Norwood, who happened to share her great love of detective fiction, as did another prominent classical scholar, Gilbert Murray, who not long before his death in 1957 informed Freeman that he had long been a great admirer of Mary Fitt.

Freeman's rise in the field of higher education during the first half of the twentieth century is particularly impressive given the facts, which were then deemed disabling, of her sex and modest family background as the daughter of a brewer's traveller, which precluded the possibility of a prestigious Oxbridge education. 'A man will do much for a woman who is his friend, but to be suspected of being a brewer's traveller… was not pleasant,' observes the mortified narrator of William Black's novel *A Princess of Thule* (1883), anxious to correct this socially damning misimpression. Evidently unashamed of her circumstances, however, Freeman evinced a lifetime ambition to reach ordinary, everyday people with her work, eschewing perpetual confinement in academe's ivory tower.

Before turning to crime writing in 1936 under the alias of Mary Fitt, Freeman published five mainstream novels and a book of short stories, beginning with *Martin Hanner: A Comedy* (1926), a well-received academic novel about a (male) classics professor who teaches at a red-brick university in northern England. After the outbreak of the Second World War, while she was still employed at the university, Freeman, drawing on her classical education, published the patriotically themed *It Has All Happened Before: What the Greeks Thought of Their Nazis* (1941).* She also lectured British soldiers headed to the Mediterranean theatre of war on the terrain, customs and language of Greece, a country she had not merely read about but visited in the Thirties. During the cold war, when Freeman, passed over for promotion, had retired from teaching to devote herself to writing in a world confronted with yet another totalitarian menace, she returned to her inspirational theme, publishing *Fighting Words from the Greeks for Today's Struggle* (1952). Perhaps her most highly regarded layman-oriented work from this period is *Greek City-States* (1950), in which, notes scholar Eleanor Irwin, Freeman uses her 'uncanny eye for settings, as is often seen in her mysteries', to bring 'the city-states to life'. Freeman explicitly drew on her interests in both classicism and crime in her

---

* Under the heading of 'Dictators', Freeman quotes Solon: 'When a man has risen too high, it is not easy to check him after; now is the time to take heed of everything.' Timeless words indeed!

much-admired book *The Murder of Herodes and Other Trials from the Athenian Law Courts* (1946), which was effusively praised by the late Jacques Barzun, another distinguished academic mystery fancier, as 'a superb book for the [crime] connoisseur'.

In spite of her classical background, Kathleen Freeman derived her 'Mary Fitt' pseudonym – which she also employed to publish juvenile fiction, including a series of books about an intrepid young girl named Annabella – not from ancient Greece but from Elizabethan England, Eleanor Irwin has hypothesised, for the name bears resemblance to that of Mary Fitton, the English gentlewoman and maid of honour who is a candidate for the 'Dark Lady' of Shakespeare's queer-inflected sonnets. Irwin points out that Freeman's 'earliest literary publications were highly personal reflections on relationships in sonnet form'. The name also lends itself to a pun – 'Miss Fitt' – which it is likely the author deliberately intended, given her droll wit and nonconformity.

While Kathleen Freeman's first four detective novels, which appeared in 1936 and 1937, are stand-alones, her fifth essay in the form, *Sky-Rocket* (1938), introduces her burly, pipe-smoking, green-eyed, red-moustached series police detective, Superintendent Mallett, who is somewhat reminiscent of Agatha Christie's occasional sleuth Superintendent Battle. The two men not only share similar builds but have similarly symbolic surnames.

Joined initially by acerbic police surgeon Dr Jones and later by the imaginative Dr Dudley 'Dodo' Fitzbrown – the latter of whom, introduced in *Expected Death* (1938), soon supersedes Jones – Superintendent Mallett would dominate Mary Fitt's mystery output over the next two decades. Only after Freeman's heart condition grew perilously grave in 1954 does it seem that the author's interest in Mallett and Fitzbrown dwindled, with the pair appearing in only two of the five novels published between 1956 and 1960. Similarly diminished in her final years was Freeman's involvement with the activities of the Detection Club, into which she initially had thrown herself with considerable zeal. In the first half of the decade she had attended club dinners with her beloved life partner, Dr Liliane Marie Catherine Clopet, persuaded Welsh polymath Bertrand Russell, an omnivorous detective-fiction reader, to speak at one of the dinners, and wrote a BBC radio play, *A Death in the Blackout* (in which Dr Fitzbrown appears), with the proceeds from the play going to the club.

Presumably Kathleen Freeman met Liliane Clopet at the University College of South Wales and Monmouthshire, where Clopet registered as a student in 1919. Precisely when the couple began cohabiting is unclear, but by 1929 Freeman had dedicated the first of what would be many books to Clopet ('For L.M.C.C.'), and by the Thirties the pair resided at Lark's Rise, the jointly owned house – including a surgery for Clopet and her patients – that the couple had built in St Mellons, a Cardiff suburb. In the author's biography on the back of her Penguin mystery reprints, Freeman noted that a friend had described the home where she lived as 'your Italian-blue house', though she elaborated: 'It is not Italian, but it is blue – sky-blue.' There Freeman would pass away and Clopet would reside for many years afterwards.

Born on 13 December 1901 in Berwick-upon-Tweed in Northumberland, Liliane Clopet was one of three children of native Frenchman Aristide Bernard Clopet, a master mariner, and his English wife Charlotte Towerson, a farmer's daughter. Although Aristide became a naturalised British citizen, the Clopets maintained close connections with France. In 1942, during the Second World War, Liliane's only brother, Karl Victor Clopet – a master mariner like his father who for a dozen years had run a salvage tug in French Morocco – was smuggled by Allied forces from Casablanca to London, where he provided details of Moroccan ports, beaches and coastal defences, which were crucially important to the victory of the United States over Vichy French forces at the ensuing Battle of Port Lyautey.

Even more heroically (albeit tragically), Liliane's cousin Evelyne Clopet served with the French Resistance and was executed by the Nazis in 1944, after British forces had parachuted her into France; at her death she was only twenty-two years old. In 1956, under another pseudonym (Caroline Cory), Kathleen Freeman published a novel set in wartime France, *Doctor Underground*, in which she drew on Evelyne's experiences. A couple of years earlier, Liliane Clopet herself had published a pseudonymous novel, *Doctor Dear*, in which she depicted a female physician's struggles with sexism among her colleagues and patients.

Kathleen Freeman, who was rather masculine-looking in both her youth and middle age (boyish in her twenties, she grew stouter over the years, wearing her hair short and donning heavy tweeds), produced no issue and at her death left her entire estate, valued at over £300,000 in today's money, to Liliane Clopet. In a letter to another correspondent she avowed: 'My books are my children and I love them dearly.' Admittedly, Freeman shared custody of her mysteries with that queer Miss Fitt, but surely she loved her criminally inclined offspring, too. I have no doubt that the author would be pleased to see these books back in print again after the passage of so many years. Readers of vintage mysteries, now eager to embrace the stylish and sophisticated country-house detective novels and psychological suspense tales of an earlier era, will doubtless be pleased as well.

CURTIS EVANS

Death and Mary Dazill

FOR
L. M. C. C.

Prologue

The three men—Superintendent Mallett, Dr. Fitzbrown and Dr. Jones—turned away from the grave, into which the workmen had begun to shovel the heavy yellow clay mixed with stones. It was a drizzling afternoon in November. They had come across from Chode to attend the funeral of the local police-sergeant; and the ceremony in the little grey church, smelling of damp stones, and at the graveside in the misty rain, had lowered their spirits considerably. Even the post-funereal ham and whisky were, for once, lacking: the dead constable seemed to have no relatives.

They threaded their way among the graves, across the wet grass towards the gravel-path. Mallett and Jones, walking in single file, kept their eyes fixed on the ground; but Fitzbrown stopped occasionally to read the name on a tombstone. The other two reached the path before him: there the Vicar of Long Marley awaited them.

'A dreary afternoon,' he called out cheerfully. 'You fellows must come back and have a cup of tea with us.' Then, as they demurred: 'Oh, come, come! My wife's expecting you.' He made off down the path toward the lych-gate; Mallett and Jones followed him resignedly.

As the Vicar reached the lych-gate, two tall old ladies entered: he swept off his hat to them, and paused for a moment to speak to them. Mallett and Jones slackened their pace, and, unwilling to be drawn into the encounter, stopped as if to wait for Fitzbrown. The two old ladies, after a few minutes' gracious conversation, bowed to the Vicar, or rather inclined their heads like two queens, and passed on. They were followed at a respectful distance by a chauffeur in wine-coloured livery: he stopped when they stopped, and moved when they moved, keeping exactly the same distance between himself and them, as if drawn by an invisible wire. He carried an enormous circular wreath of hothouse flowers: arum lilies, scarlet amaryllis, gardenias.

The little procession swept past Mallett and Jones, leaving the heavy scent of the wreath hanging on the November air. The two men, a little curious by now, watched them as they turned off up a side-path and halted in front of an enormous piece of statuary, the most conspicuous object in the whole churchyard, a broken column of white marble, on a pedestal, with, in front of it, a railed-in 'garden' of white chipped stones. The two old ladies, upright as the marble column, and in their black clothes just as conspicuous, took up their stations one on each side of the low railing, while the chauffeur, at a gesture from one of them, placed the wreath at the foot of the pedestal. All three stood for a moment as if to attention; then the procession returned along the way it had come. Mallett and Jones stood on one side to let them pass by.

Fitzbrown had now emerged on to the path. The other two watched him as he crossed it, and, to their surprise, went over to look at the massive marble tomb with its new ornament of flowers. He bent down, hands on knees, to look at the inscription… A few minutes later he joined them.

'I should have thought you saw enough of corpses without wanting to pursue them below ground," grumbled Dr. Jones. 'When a man's dead, he's dead.'

Fitzbrown stamped, to get the clay and grass off his boots.

'But his soul goes marching on,' he said, 'or rather, his memory, if you prefer. Sometimes, that is.—Did you notice that little ceremony going on away back there just now? Intriguing, wasn't it?'

'Pooh,' said Jones, 'you don't mean to say a man's continued existence, or even his "memory" as you call it, depends on the size and price of the wreaths his relatives lay on his grave?'

'Not exactly,' said Fitzbrown. 'For all I know, one of these graves that nobody bothers about, with no name on it or just a headstone with a name, may contain the earthly envelope of some immortal mind or idea. But—when you see an enormous wreath being laid on a tomb, you assume that the person's recently dead, don't you? Well, I went to look at the inscription on that one— and you may be surprised to hear, the last person was buried in it *nearly fifty years ago.*'

'H'm,' said Mallett. 'Pretty good. What was the name; did you notice?'

'De Boulter,' said Fitzbrown. 'There were two inmates—father and son. The son died first, aged twenty. The father died just six months later, aged forty-six. Things like that always set my mind working. One scents a story. It's an odd name, too. But this churchyard's full of odd names.'

They had reached the lych-gate. The Vicar was waiting for them. He had just, apparently, replaced his hat after waving farewell to the two old ladies, as their long black saloon car moved softly away. The Vicar stood gazing after them for a moment, as if reluctant to see the last of them. He turned, however, with renewed gusto to his three guests.

'This way, this way,' he said, 'just across the road. The samovar, and Mrs. Barratt, will be waiting.'

The vicarage sitting-room smelt of old books and tobacco, and not a little dust. But it was comfortable. There was a blazing fire, and deep chairs for all. The Vicar's wife beamed, and encouraged her husband to tell stories. Gradually the three visitors thawed, stretched out their legs and felt at their ease. Pipes were lighted, and a silence fell. Mrs. Barratt, having served her purpose as dispenser of tea and toast, was about to leave them, when a sudden question from Fitzbrown arrested her; though it was to the Vicar, and not to her, that he spoke.

'Who *were* those two old ladies with the lily-wreath?'

The Vicar blinked several times rapidly; for the abruptness of Fitzbrown's question clearly showed that he had been brooding on that scene in the churchyard, not listening to the Vicar's stories. But the Vicar was used to such things; he made a quick recovery, for he scented the possibility of an even longer chain of anecdotes. He sat forward, hands on knees:

'Those were two of my most difficult—patients, Doctor, I'd say if I were you.' He rubbed his knees, then thumped them one by one: 'Yes. Those were the Misses de Boulter, of Chetwode Lodge, half a mile from here—Lindy and Arry, to each other and their intimates, if they had any: by christening, Lindisfarne and Arran.'

'Lindisfarne and Arran?' echoed Fitzbrown. 'Names of islands?'

'Quite so,' said the Vicar, beaming as if he himself were responsible for the phenomenon that evoked so much interest. 'Their father was a remarkable man, I believe. It's he that is buried in that vault with the marble column, in our churchyard. He died when those two were young girls scarcely out of their 'teens; and that's half a century ago. Yet every week—every *week*—winter and summer, they bring a wreath like the one you saw, and place it on the tomb.'

'Then the young man buried there must be their brother?'

'Yes.'

The Vicar cast an odd, sidelong look at his wife, who still stood there listening. It was as if he were asking her: 'Is it wise to evoke these memories—to raise these ghosts—after all these years?' But he evidently saw nothing forbidding in her answering look, for he turned back to Fitzbrown and said, almost invitingly: 'It's a long story.' He caught Mallett's inquiring glance, also fixed upon him, and added: 'If it had happened now, it would have been just in your line, Superintendent. But as things were, it remained—and remains—unsolved.'

Mallett's red moustache bristled. 'Unsolved?' he repeated. The word, to him, was like the sound of a bugle to a war-horse.

'Yes. Unsolved. A mystery. It happened fifty years ago—and people's memories are short, very, very short. Life nowadays is full of sensations: old stories are forgotten. But there are still some who remember... Tell me, did you ever hear the name of—Mary Dazill?'

There was a moment's silence. Then 'Mary Dazill?' said Fitzbrown sharply. 'Why—I know that name! I saw it only to-day—this afternoon. It was on a little headstone, sunk in the grass. I noticed it because it had only the name and the date. The date!' he said excitedly. 'It was the same—the same as on that tomb!'

The soft voice of Mrs. Barrett corrected him. 'A year later,' she said.

'Yes, yes, maybe,' said Fitzbrown impatiently. 'I mean, they were all around 1890.' He rounded on her. 'You don't mean to say those deaths were connected? The little headstone I saw was on the other side of the churchyard, as far away as possible from the de Boulters' tomb.'

Mrs. Barratt nodded. 'Naturally. Believe me, there was every reason why it should be.'

Attention was now concentrated on her. The circle was widened to admit her. But she still stood there, as if about to go.

'Nobody knows the truth of the story,' put in the Vicar eagerly. 'But my wife knows more about it than anyone, I suppose. She was not yet born when it happened: but she had it from her mother, who knew the de Boulter girls well. Strangely enough her mother's father was the incumbent here at the time.'

'Yes,' said Mrs. Barratt. 'I always said I'd never marry into the Church.' She laughed softly.

The Vicar spoke impulsively. 'Bring the old photo-album, my dear,' he said; and to Fitzbrown: 'There are photos of the de Boulter family—father, son, and daughters—on horseback—in a boat—sitting all together on the lawn… there's even,' he lowered his voice, 'a photo of Mary Dazill.'

Again there was a silence at the name. It sounded ominous, no one knew why, unless it was that it conjured up the picture Fitzbrown had drawn, of a lonely grave marked by a headstone bearing only a name and a date; and on the other side of the church-yard, as far away as possible, the proud marble column, tall yet broken, of the de Boulter tomb.

'Yes,' said Mrs. Barratt, 'there's a photo of Mary Dazill. She was a very beautiful woman, by any standard, past or present.' But still she made no move to fetch the photograph-album.

It was Mallett who said at last: 'Won't you tell us the story? We're all curious; and my friend Dr. Fitzbrown here is completely captivated.' He turned to Fitzbrown: 'You mustn't fall in love with a phantom, you know. One has heard of such things.'

Dr. Jones gave a snort.

Mrs. Barratt turned to him quickly. 'You don't believe in the power of the dead, Doctor? You don't believe that, whatever happens to their poor souls, their influence reaches out of the past—their loves, their hatreds, live on and touch the living?'

Jones, taken aback, muttered something hostile to this idea. But Mrs. Barratt took no notice: her plain, ruddy face shone in the firelight, her brown eyes glowed, and her voice was warm with the selfless interest of one who finds it easier to live in other people's lives than to devise one of her own.

'Those two women you saw just now,' she said, 'Lindy and Arran de Boulter—they are living and walking monuments to the power of Mary Dazill. In the struggle that there was between them they destroyed her—'

'Ah, don't say that, Lucy!' put in the Vicar, raising an agonised hand.

'They destroyed her,' repeated Lucy, 'one way or another: what does it matter whether that's literally true, or not? They had to, to save themselves. But—in doing so, they chained themselves to her for ever.'

'But,' said Fitzbrown, 'there were no flowers on the other grave.'

'No,' agreed Mrs. Barratt. 'And the wreaths on their grave get bigger and bigger—don't they, James?—James feels it's almost wicked,' she said with a laugh, 'to see such exotic flowers, week after week—unseemly, or worldly—anyway, not suitable to our modest little village graveyard. But hints produce no effect. I think he'd forgive them—wouldn't you, dear?—if only they'd put one lily, or even a bunch of violets, on the grave of Mary Dazill.'

The Vicar bowed his head, as if caught out in a weakness.

'Perhaps some day they will,' suggested Fitzbrown to console him.

The Vicar shook his head. 'Never. But tell your story, my dear. You can see these gentlemen are interested. As I've told you, nobody knows the whole story, except those who took part in it—but my wife will tell you all that's known. By the way, did you read the inscription on the tomb?'

'I did,' said Fitzbrown. 'It impressed me—but it struck me as very unusual—I might almost say, un-Christian. It's a harsh note, a hard, clear note, if you'll excuse me, Vicar, among all those limping verses and pious phrases.'

'It's not Christian,' said the Vicar. 'It's pagan. It's from an old Greek writer, who lived three hundred years before Christ. My wife's grandfather, I'm told, strenuously opposed their choice; but at last, seeing their determination, and not having my real power to prevent their using what, after all, is a perfectly moral sentiment, though it lacks the Christian message of hope—'

'What is the inscription?' said Dr. Jones curiously.

'It runs like this.' The Vicar sat back, and placing his finger-tips together, quoted from memory:

'"Being human, never ask Heaven for a life free from sorrow; ask rather for courage to endure." It comes from the Greek poet Menander. My wife's grandfather, as I was saying, did his best to prevent their using it; but at last he gave way, on condition that the name of the author should not be given. And there it stays. One can't deny its suitability—though one could have wished—But tell your story, my dear, as far as it goes. As for the whole truth, that will never be known.'

Book 1

I

'The day she arrived,' began Mrs. Barratt, 'I remember my mother telling me, was a lovely day in spring. Chetwode Lodge was like fairyland in those days. The main entrance faced north; and on the south side the lawns sloped gently down to a little private bridge over the stream; and beyond that, several miles away as the crow flies, was the sea. These things are all still true, of course; but nowadays, when people can go about more, gardens aren't as important as they used to be. The gardens at Chetwode Lodge are still lovely; but they're kept up more as a convention than because they're part of the life of the people who live there. From my mother's description, I get the distinct impression that they had a quality—a beauty—which is lost now.'

'That's because it's in the past,' put in Dr. Jones.

'Partly, perhaps,' said Mrs. Barratt. 'But from my mother's description, I gathered something more...' She turned over the thick cardboard pages of the photograph-album, and pointed to a faded brown print. 'That was taken in the garden, under the cedar-tree. The girls have their long white summer frocks on, all frills and flounces. The one in the chair is Lindy, I think'—she peered closely—'and the one sitting at her feet is Arran, with the big bow on the back of her head. Lindy is a year older—and she was always the leader—still is. She was the bold, proud one—black hair, black eyes, scornful ways. Arran was quieter, with soft brown hair and blue eyes—but she wasn't meek, either. Perhaps she was, in the last resort, the more unyielding of the two.'

'Who's the handsome buck in the blazer, leaning against the tree-trunk?' said Fitzbrown. 'He should be called Edward. Is that their brother?' he added more seriously, remembering the marble tomb with its inscription, "Aged 20 years."

'No,' said Mrs. Barratt, 'that's John Despenser. He came of a neighbouring family that left these parts many years ago. He was at Oxford with their only brother, Leonard de Boulter, who was his junior, I believe, by about a year. At that time John Despenser was a welcome visitor to the house. He was courting Lindy, with everybody's approval, and it was merely a matter of arrangement between the families when the engagement should be announced.'

'And how old,' said Fitzbrown, 'was Lindy at that time?' He peered again at the photo, but could make out nothing of the features of the girl sitting in the wicker-work garden chair.

'She was about eighteen,' said Mrs. Barratt. 'The two girls had spent most of their lives at a boarding-school, while their parents were in Burma. Mrs. de Boulter died out there, seven or eight years before her husband came home to stay. The old house was opened up—the girls were withdrawn from school—everything came to life again. But Mr. de Boulter had strange ideas for those times: he didn't expect his daughters to look after him—he had lived for so long out East that to him it seemed improper for a white woman to soil her hands—and yet, though he found them decorative and full of character, he was highly dissatisfied with their education. I remember, my mother said he used to say that intellectually they were a pair of untutored savages, when they first came home from their expensive south-coast boarding school. They had the manners of gentlewomen; but as for knowledge, an understanding of the universe they lived in, they were of the Neolithic age. He also said that they were full of tribal superstitions about caste and rites—social rites; for as he had been about the world a good deal, and observed other races, certain of our English customs seemed to him to be no less "tribal" than those of India or Burma... Well, he couldn't, in those days, send them to a university as he had their brother; and he didn't want to lose their society, so soon after recovering them, by sending them to a finishing school. So he decided that their education must continue at home.

'The first step was to secure a private tutor. Being a man, he had an instinctive antipathy towards having another male in the house. It was easy to find reasons of convenience for appointing a woman.

'This woman was Mary Dazill.'

2

'Well, but where did your father find her?' said John, lounging against the trunk of the cedar-tree, which stretched out its long, dark-green, fan-like branches protectingly over the round table.

'We don't know,' said Lindy, 'we don't know at all. She was recommended by someone—a certain Lady Millborn, with whom he's very friendly. They've corresponded for many years, ever since my father was a young man; and he takes her advice on everything.'

'Lady Millborn?' said John. 'I seem to know the name.'

'Oh, yes, she is a great social figure—though not in favour at Court, I believe. She's an old woman of sixty-five or so, but he obviously still finds her attractive.' Lindy laughed. 'I feel sure she must have been his first love, though she's twenty years older.'

John gazed round the lovely garden, and over his shoulder to the house, whose red-brick walls glowed in the afternoon sunshine. 'I wonder,' he said, 'if your father will marry again, now he's come home?'

Lindy shot a look at him from under her dark brows.

'Don't be absurd, John! At his age? And Lady Millborn—'

'I wasn't thinking of Lady Millborn,' said John. He came and sat down beside her, in the other wicker chair. 'You don't seem to realise that your father's still a young man, from most points of view—marriage, for instance.' He spoke with a gravity beyond his years.

Lindy's dark eyes flashed, and she said scornfully:

'I hope *you* don't think forty-five the best time in life for a man to marry!'

John laughed: it was possible to hear a note of embarrassment in his laughter. 'Of course not, Lindy! But it's *one* of the times—'

'My father has been married already!' said Lindy hotly.

'I know that. You see, Lindy, one of his lives is over; his life with your mother, his first life, his youth. Now that's made doubly clear to him, because he has changed his habitat as well: he has left Burma and all it stood for—probably far more than we know—'

Lindy's glance was still wrathful; but he took no notice.

'And here he is, in England—in the country, with nothing to do but lead a gentleman's life, surrounded by his horses, his dogs, his servants and—his daughters.'

'John, you are intolerable!' cried Lindy. Neither of them noticed Arran, who had come quietly across the lawn, and now stood behind them, holding against her cheek a curious little bundle of white fur.

'Father doesn't regard us as ornaments merely! We mean a great deal to him. He has said so, to us both. He has said he regards us as more than his daughters—as his friends. He would never—'

John went on inexorably. 'Daughters aren't enough for a man, Lindy—no, nor even friends. Have you ever really looked at your father? To you, of course, forty and onwards is a great age; to me, too, in a way. But I can see him from another angle—his own. From that point of view, I assure you, he's as young as we are—just as curious about life, just as eager for new experiences. Perhaps more so—because he's not afraid, as we are—' His handsome face clouded.

'Afraid!' echoed Lindy contemptuously. 'What is there to be afraid of?' She leaned forward to look at him. 'You don't mean to say *you* are afraid of anything, John? I don't believe it.'

John shrugged his shoulders. 'Oh, I don't mean of things physical. I suppose I'd make as good a soldier as most men if ever England were at war. But—it's the mental experiences that terrify me—the mistakes one can make—the awful, inescapable mistakes—and life is so short—'

The sudden pain in his voice made Lindy turn to look at him even more closely. The quiet voice of Arran made both of them start.

'I'm sorry to interrupt you; but I came to tell you the train's in. I saw the smoke from my window.' She looked back to the house; on the south-east wing was a tower, capped with red tiles, where Arran had her bedroom. 'So they won't be many minutes now.'

'Has Baxter gone to fetch her?' said Lindy. 'Did Father tell him? He said nothing to me.'

'No,' said Arran, stroking the fluffy white animal and looking down at it, 'he has gone himself. I saw him driving the dog-cart, ten minutes ago.'

Lindy said nothing for a moment. She brooded, a puzzled frown on her young forehead. John got up and stood behind his chair near Arran. 'What's that you've got there?' he said, putting out a tentative hand, but withholding it some inches away. 'It looks like a little white monkey. What a high brow it has! And I say! What wonderful blue eyes! Why, they're a shade more blue than yours, Arry! What is it? A kitten?'

'Yes, a kitten,' said Arran. John's hand lowered, then stroked the kitten where it lay on her breast. 'It's a Siamese kitten. Father brought back two Siamese cats with him, from Burma. They wouldn't let him have them at first, in case they were diseased—they kept them at the Customs. But yesterday they arrived by train—and with them four of these! They're very valuable. And aren't they sweet?' She turned the kitten's face up to hers, and in doing so, touched John's hand. John saw the blush that swept up her neck and face; and he let his hand remain there. After all, Lindy could not see.

'When he grows up,' went on Arran rather breathlessly, 'he will not be white any longer, but pale fawn, and his tail and paws and ears and face—mask, Father says one should call it—will turn chocolate brown. But his eyes will always be as blue as the sea in summer—'

'He squints most shockingly,' said John, stooping as if to peer at the kitten more closely. The fine hair of Arran's bent head touched his forehead like a cobweb. 'Are you sure there's nothing wrong with his eyes?'

'No, no, it's his nature!' said Arran. 'And look—he has a little kink at the end of his tail. It is a mark of his royal breeding, so Father says.'

John felt the kitten's tail-tip; but this time Arran withdrew her hand. She left him standing there, and crossing in front of Lindy, sat down in the wicker chair John had vacated.

'What do you suppose she'll be like?' said Lindy. 'How funny of Father to go himself to meet her! He is so lazy as a rule.'

'Perhaps Baxter had work to do in the garden,' said Arran absently, running her fingers down the kitten's spine.

'Six feet two, like a grenadier,' interposed John with false heartiness, 'dressed in black—spectacles. Carries an umbrella and wears elastic-sided boots. Has a special penchant for arithmetic...'

Lindy got up. 'Excuse me—I must go and see that her room is ready.' She went off quickly across the lawn.

John came and sat in her chair, beside Arran. He made as if to stroke the kitten again, but Arran drew back. John also withdrew as if hurt or offended:

'Why are you so cold to me, Arry?' he said in a low urgent tone. 'It's not often I see you alone.'

Arran bit her lip. 'Must you spoil everything?' she said. 'I don't understand you. Are you trying to show me up as completely—disloyal?'

John smiled at her lazily, from where he lay in the long chair. 'How solemn you are!' he said. 'Sweet seventeen—and never—" He leaned forward quickly. 'Some day, Arry, when I catch you in the rose-garden—or between the yew hedges—we shall change all that.'

He expected her to get up and leave him, in a whirl of white frills and flounces. But she sat there motionless, with her head half-turned away. She had forgotten even to hold the kitten closely, and feeling himself neglected, he arched his back, pressed against her, and finally jumped down.

'Why don't you answer me, Arry?' persisted John, tormenting her. 'Why don't you protest, as a well-brought-up girl should? Or didn't they teach you what to do in such circumstances, at your boarding-school? Perhaps the new governess—or tutor, or tutrix, should I call her?—will tell you!'

Arran turned sharply on him. 'You enjoy hurting me—making me despise myself even more than I do. I wonder why.' Her voice was low, and her lips scarcely moved; but the anger in her eyes made them seem a darker blue.

'Why shouldn't I?' he answered hotly. '*I* am hurt. *I* am in torment. Why should *you* be spared? Why should I protect—everybody? Oh, yes, I know the convention: one must let oneself be devoured alive, by a tiger, by a demon, rather than cause a lady a moment's inconvenience! But you see, I don't subscribe to that view. I think you should look after yourselves a little more. What am *I* made of?—iron or granite?—that I should bear your miseries for you, as well as my own?'

'You can't,' said Arran, in a voice so low that he could scarcely hear. But his hearing was acute enough, then, to catch every shade of Arran's voice. He leaned forward and said, with his lips almost touching her hair:

'Forgive me, darling. I can't help it. I love you.'

'John,' murmured Arran, 'you *must* tell Lindy.'

'Tell Lindy? Arran, darling, I can't. You know that. She—I'm engaged to her. It's not announced—but I've spoken to your father. I've spoken to *her*. My people know. That's what torments me.' He struck his forehead, while Arran watched him, her expression hardening to an unhappy scepticism. 'Oh, why was I so blind? You were there—and somehow I never saw you till it was too late.'

Arran had recovered her calm. 'The others will be here in a minute,' she said. 'I think I can hear the dog-cart. Perhaps, as you say, Miss Dazill will solve the problem for us—by never letting us out of her sight. She will let you see Lindy, no doubt, as you are engaged to marry her. But as for me—' she laughed, and her youthful scorn was like a blow in the face to him.

He got up angrily. 'I'm going, Arry. Please tell Lindy I've remembered—I promised to see Pratt about a fishing-rod. Tell her I'll be here in the morning—to say good-bye.'

'Good-bye?' repeated Arran.

'Yes—good-bye. I could have stayed till Thursday—but what's the use? The sooner I go, the easier for both of us.'

Arran looked up, fully aware of his attempt to beguile her, yet not strong enough to resist it altogether. 'Don't go John,' she said, to please him rather than because she wanted him to stay. 'Don't go for my sake, that is. It will pass. I can bear it. I shall find something to distract me. I shall work hard—'

'If I stay,' said John, kneeling on the arm of the chair, 'will you meet me in the rose-garden to-morrow, just to say good-bye? Only for a moment, Arry—you can't refuse me that. I promise you, this time it *will* be good-bye—forever. I shall come back cured—or I shall not come back at all.'

Arran did not believe him in the slightest. But her will-power seemed numbed as he urged her:

'To-morrow, in the rose-garden, at three. I happen to know Lindy is going with my mother, to see the dressmaker. You'll be here alone. I shall come over when I've seen them safely off there. They'll be an hour at least. You will?'

'And Miss Dazill?' faltered Arry. 'The new—governess? How am to I know what *she'll* see fit to do? She may want to take me walking, or set me working, to-morrow. Oh, how absurd of Father, to put us in charge of a governess, at our age!'

'You can get rid of her,' pleaded John. 'She'll want to rest—at her age, she will like to sleep in the afternoon. You will? Promise!'

Arran cast a hasty glance at the house. 'Yes, yes. Please go now, John. I can see them coming.'

John, too, looked, and could see movement on the terrace. But the protecting branch of the cedar still served him well. He kissed her, quickly and lightly, on the lips, and strode off across the lawn…

And so, that first day, he did not see Mary Dazill, though she saw him, and wondered who he was, and why he was hurrying away.

3

The dog-cart bowled down the flat country road, between the tall overarching elms, at a smart speed. It was a smart turn-out altogether: the chestnut pony's coat glistened, and he arched his neck, with its close-cut mane, as he high-stepped his way along. The newly varnished body of the dog-cart glistened too. And the man who held the reins in his yellow-gloved hands was in keeping with his vehicle: upright, square-shouldered, elbows to sides, he sat as if he were driving a tandem, not a little toy he had bought for the amusement of his daughters and their governess. But at that time, the pride of life and vigour that were in him would not allow him to do anything otherwise than well.

Ralph de Boulter was enjoying this period of his life as he had never enjoyed anything before. He had not expected to; he had expected to find English country life dull, and to feel a certain nostalgia for the East. But the nostalgia that he felt was merely an added pleasure: it was of the romantic sort, which left out all annoyances and discomforts from the picture, and conjured up only the colour and charm of his Burmese existence. True, he had left his wife there, in the English cemetery at Rangoon; but the truth—though he did not tell himself this quite openly—was that this suited him very well. He had been fond of her, and proud of her, while she lived; but he had a horror of death, or rather, of the ritual connected with it; and it was a relief to him not to have to think, even, any longer about a grave. The grave was on the other side of the world, and he paid a subscription to have it looked after in perpetuity; it would have weighed round his neck like a millstone if it had been situated in the local graveyard, where he would have had to visit it every time he went to church. Sometimes he dreamt that this was so, and woke up troubled; but during the day he hardly gave it a thought. He had already arranged to have a memorial plaque put up on the church wall; and that ended the matter. One could dismiss it from one's mind. On a day like this, when the sun shone, and the birds were singing, and the orchards were white with blossom of cherry and pear, it would be folly, almost ingratitude, to think of death.

And now, he was driving to meet Mary Dazill.

He smiled to himself, a little self-consciously, at what he was doing. It was a little unusual for the master of the house to go himself to meet his daughters' governess. He could imagine the sharp look Lindy would give him if she knew. He prided himself on being really the master, though the very antithesis of a tyrant; but a less strong-minded man would have been already a little afraid of Lindy, with her quick eye and ready tongue. He thought for a moment of his two daughters, Lindy, so strong-minded, Arran, so gentle: he doubted if John Despenser would make the best husband for Lindy... However, that was his affair. He thought of his son Leonard, at present a complete mystery to him, though even he could feel his extraordinary charm... But his thoughts shied, as they always did, at the thought of Leonard... Leonard, the only thing in his present new life, which made him feel middle-aged, *passé*, of a different world...

He passed a high-hedged garden, and caught the delicious scent of narcissi. On the other hand, running along at the side of the road, was a clear brook rippling over stones; the rhythmic sharp click of the pony's hooves on the road, and the soft burr of the rubber-tyred wheels, did not drown the gurglings and babblings of the brook as it accompanied him... Why was he meeting Mary Dazill? What possible interest could she be to him, except in so far as he cared—and he certainly cared a great deal—about his daughters' education?

His moustache twitched as he thought of Lady Millborn: she believed she had outwitted him. He had gone to her, once again, for advice; she had looked at him, decided at once to kill two birds with one stone. 'The day of the duenna is over,' she had assured him. 'What you need is a woman—older, of course, more mature, more settled: but not a gorgon or a gargoyle! It's not good for young girls to be continually in the company of a failure. How can she teach them anything when they have her before them as a warning?' Lady Millborn laughed. 'I know exactly what you want, my dear Ralph, for your daughters. You want them to retain all their feminine charm, without being nincompoops. You'd like them to have a *reasonable* knowledge of themselves and of the world they live in, instead of the mass of prejudices and superstitions thought proper for girls; but you do want them to retain a sense of proportion.' She laughed again. 'I sympathise with you. It's just what I should have liked myself. I'm clever, as you know: but in my young days, it would have meant social ostracism to admit it, so all my arts had to be expended in concealing it. So I married a man without a brain in his head, and my own daughters are nincompoops! But yours evidently are not; and there's no reason why they should pretend to be. Times are changing—I can see it coming, inevitably, though it's a long way off yet.'

So she talked on, clarifying ideals which he held obscurely. But with Lady Millborn, an ideal was—however sincerely felt—not discussed for its own sake merely. She came to the point. 'Now—I know of someone who'd be exactly the right companion for your girls. She is cultured, travelled, charming—and unfortunate. Her name is Mary Dazill.'

'Dazill?' echoed Ralph. 'Haven't I heard that name somewhere?'

'You certainly have,' said Lady Millborn, 'unless you've been asleep for the last five years.—Oh, but of course, you were away all that time—perhaps you didn't see the English papers!'

'We saw them,' said Ralph, 'a couple of months late—sometimes longer when we were up-country. Why?'

Lady Millborn lowered her voice. 'There was a scandal—over her mother. It was a *cause célèbre*—though nowadays when there's always so much news, these cases aren't what they used to be. Her mother was on the stage—an opera-singer, I believe—a woman of quite good family, but—well, she married Rupert Dazill, who was a nephew of the Marquis of Wastdale—a dreadful rotter, my dear. He ceased to live with her, soon after Mary was born, though he provided for them handsomely, I will say that for him, and Mary had an excellent education. But the mother, who doted on Rupert in spite of everything, never gave up trying to get him back. She pestered him so much that he used to disappear, for years on end. Then he'd return, hoping that she'd given up and become resigned—but not in the least! As soon as she'd hear where he was, she'd be after him. She absolutely refused to give up her claim on him; he used to get served with orders for restitution of conjugal rights and so on. In fact, she made a laughing-stock of him, by turning up at his club, at house-parties and so on.——Mary saw nothing of all this: she was at boarding-school, then she was sent abroad. But as for the mother—the thing became notorious. People took sides: she had her following, who remembered that after all the poor woman *was* his wife. And that sometimes made things rather unpleasant for Rupert. People objected to the notoriety—and to the inconvenience and embarrassment. What nobody realised was—her thwarted affections had turned her brain.

'One day, when Rupert was in London, Mrs. Dazill found out, as she always managed to do, where he was staying. She went to the hotel. There was a woman with him. Mrs. Dazill drew out a revolver from her muff, and shot them both dead.

'She was tried, of course. The prosecution did their best to prove that she had planned to harm him for years. But popular sympathy was on her side. The jury found her Guilty but Insane. She died a year later. Meanwhile—there was Mary.

'She had to come home. She had to set about earning her living. But very few people would employ her, in any capacity; and those who did made her suffer for her mother's misfortune. Some of us, who knew her mother, have tried to help her; we've tided her over the worst periods. But—Ralph, she needs a home, somewhere in which to settle down and forget... She's accomplished—a brilliant musician, a good horsewoman; she can speak French, German, and Italian like a native; and she's Wastdale's great-niece, though the family ignores her. In years, she's not so very much older than your own girls—about twenty-five, I believe. But—well, her life hasn't been gay for the past five years. She knows the world for what it is—and yet she's young enough to be a companion to them.'

Ralph listened, and did not answer at once. From the urgency in Lady Millborn's voice, he gathered that even now she had not told him all she planned for Mary. Great-niece of the Marquis of Wastdale—accomplished—beautiful—had she said that Mary was beautiful, or was that just the impression she had conveyed?—And, on the other hand, a widower, rich, still young; a man who had seen the world, who would not be frightened off by a scandal of which the chief victim was innocent, who would snap his fingers in the face of London society, if need be; who was well able to take care of any woman... Ralph read all her thoughts. He kept her waiting for a while; then he said:

'My dear Augusta, if *you* sponsor her, it is enough.'

'You'll take her?' Lady Millborn in jubilation clasped both his hands.

'Oh, I won't go so far as *that*,' said Ralph, smiling. Then, seeing her face fall, he added, 'I mean, the last word depends on my daughters.'

'On your daughters!' Lady Millborn looked amazed.

'Yes. After all, I can't impose a *companion* on them'—he emphasised the word slightly—'if they don't like her, can I? If she were an elderly gorgon, it wouldn't matter. But with a young woman, there would be trouble if their temperaments happened to clash.'

'Mary is the soul of tact,' put in Lady Millborn eagerly.

'Perhaps. But Lindy isn't.—Leave it to me, Augusta. Send Miss Dazill down to Chetwode one day next week, and meanwhile I'll break the news to the girls. If they get on well together, it might be an excellent arrangement. We'll leave it at that.'

But he had not broken it to the girls. They had no idea what was in store for them. Pusillanimous? Perhaps; but women are kittle cattle.

The dog-cart bowled into the station yard. Ralph threw the reins to one of the men standing there and walked on to the platform. The signal was down. And there, in the distance, a black speck on the converging rails, he could see the engine approaching up the incline. The puffs of white steam from its funnel seemed to synchronise with the strong beating of his heart.

4

Mary Dazill settled down very quickly among them, like a smooth stone that is placed on the surface of a pool and sinks out of sight with hardly a disturbance of the waters. She seemed determined that they should hardly notice her presence. It had been arranged that, as she was of gentle birth and rather a companion to the two girls than a governess, she should take all her meals with the family. She did so: but afterwards, she would either efface herself, or ask for permission to retire; and the family were left noticing the gap and wondering what they could do to detain her. The more she avoided them the greater the hold she gained on their thoughts. Less than a week had passed when, although she had had no personal conversation with any of them, each one was profoundly aware of the difference her coming had made.

It took them some little while to get over the shock of seeing her. Ralph, waiting on the platform, his bosom swelling with male pride at the thought that there was approaching a woman for his inspection, had formed a fairly clear picture of what she would be like. With simple cunning he believed himself to have seen through Lady Millborn: well, if Lady Millborn was offering him a wife, she would take care to consider his taste. The girl she would send would be tall, well proportioned—not stout, but a fine figure of a woman; not horsey or masculine, but a woman of whom one could be proud. True, Ralph de Boulter's first wife had been of average height only and rather slim; but Ralph's own boyish fantasies had always envisaged a Juno. He had forgotten that Lady Millborn could not possibly know this.

It was, therefore, a great surprise to him when Mary Dazill, the only passenger to alight, stepped on to the platform. She came straight up to him and gave him her gloved hand; but although he bent down to catch her greeting, he heard only a low murmur from under the brim of her hat, and he could not see her face at all. She carried nothing. He glanced back and saw the porter and the guard struggling with a large black cabin-trunk, much bulkier than its owner. The trunk seemed to be covered with foreign labels.

The train gave a screech and continued its easy-going way. Ralph conducted Miss Dazill to the dog-cart. He felt singularly foolish. He tried to tell himself that he was relieved, since here was no menace to his widowerhood, and he could continue enjoying his single state, his freedom, his easy country existence. But actually he felt disappointed, almost cheated; and mixed with this was thankfulness that no one could ever possibly know what he had been thinking. An entirely unjustifiable resentment against his old friend Lady Millborn burned in him: why had she misled him?

He helped Miss Dazill up into the dog-cart; and for some minutes they drove in silence. Mary Dazill sat with folded hands, obviously with no intention of trying to please. Ralph, uncomfortable at her nearness—for in the little dog-cart her knees brushed against his—irritated at his mistake, was for once at a loss. He stared ahead at the country lane, and wished the drive was over. At last, aware that she was neither looking ahead nor studying the scenery, but staring straight past him across his shoulder, he turned for the first time to look at her. And again a *frisson* of surprise shot through him: for under the brim of the concealing hat was a face of pearl-like beauty: small, clear-cut, delicate as china. The eyes were dark blue, fringed with black eyelashes; the nose was fine and small, the mouth small and soft-looking—the often-read but never before seen 'like a rosebud' sprang to his mind—and the whole colouring pale, tinged with the most delicate pink on the cheeks. The forehead was high, in proportion to the face, and the eyebrows very fine, long and dark... He could not see her hair.

Ralph stared at her for so long that he took in every detail: he might have been gazing at a mask. And she, though she must have been aware of his scrutiny, ignored it. She was facing him, yet her gaze passed him by; she was looking out beyond him, perhaps at the passing country, perhaps at nothing. He was so absorbed that when at last she moved he was startled and hastily looked away. He was conscious of a hot rush of colour to his neck and face—a blush, a thing he wouldn't have thought possible, at his age! Yet all that Mary Dazill had done was to draw off one of her gloves and lay the ungloved hand in her lap again. Impelled by a kind of fascination, Ralph de Boulter turned to look at the hand. It was very small, very white, without jewellery, and motionless. It looked like a hand made of porcelain.

There was a thudding of horses' hooves behind them, on the grass verge of the road. A horseman on a handsome bay overtook them at a gallop and drew up alongside. Ralph stopped the dog-cart.

'Miss Dazill,' he said, 'may I present my son Leonard?'

Leonard, stooping down from his superior height, smiled at Mary and held out his hand. She gave him her ungloved hand; and she, too, smiled, for the first time.

'We shall meet later,' said Leonard. 'I'll ride ahead and tell them you're coming.'

He gave his horse a touch with his riding-crop, and off they both flew, along the road and out of sight round a bend.

Ralph drove on, feeling suddenly middle-aged.

5

Leonard de Boulter,' said Mrs. Barratt bending over the album,' was admitted by everybody to be charming. It's a much-abused word; but what other word is there? I've heard my mother try to put into words the nature of his charm: she said once, he was like sunshine; another time, she said he was like a day in spring. I've always thought,' she added, 'that she herself was a little in love with him. But'—she cast a quick look at her husband—'that, of course, was before she met my father.' She paused, and turned over a page. 'She also said that, like sunshine, Leonard was elusive. He was not unsatisfactory, ever—but he seemed to come and go at will. One would not count on his being there—or *not* being there, either. I am glad there is no photograph of Leonard I can show you.

'But there are plenty of photos of Lindy.'

Lindy came down the stairs, prepared to be condescending. She herself regarded this idea of a companion-governess as one of the absurd notions natural to fathers. But she loved her father deeply, and was willing to accept whatever came from him in the spirit in which it was meant. She really believed that he cared above all things for the welfare of herself and her sister and brother; and if he had strange ways of trying to ensure their welfare, that was because he had been away for so long, and knew so little about them. She did not think that she and Arran needed a governess, and she was quite sure they didn't need a companion. But she was prepared to let the experiment take its course, for the inevitable six months or more, until it became obviously otiose. What did one teacher more matter to one who had been at a boarding-school, surrounded by teachers? And then there was John. Soon their engagement would be announced—and then, a few more pianoforte lessons perhaps, and a little elementary book-keeping, would be all anybody could possibly require her to learn. She needed no instructor in how to manage her life as a fiancée, a bride, a married woman. She was already in full command of herself and her resources, in fact, of all her destiny.

Tea was served in the drawing-room. When Lindy took her place at the table before the massive silver teapot, no one else had arrived. She glanced through the open french window and could see the empty chairs of that earlier party under the cedar tree. John had perhaps not waited; but where was Arran? The door opened and Leonard entered.

'Has she arrived?' said Lindy urgently.

Leonard paused a moment before speaking: 'Oh, yes, she's arrived.'

'You've seen her?'

'Oh, yes, I've seen her.'

Lindy bit her lip; she would not display the curiosity which, to her annoyance, she could not help feeling. She liked always to preserve her dignity, in her own eyes; that was why she had deliberately gone off to a different part of the house, from which the drive and the entrance-porch could not be seen. She would not allow herself to peep from upstairs windows. Leonard was at his most provoking; he seemed unaware of what was expected of him. He moved about the room, picking up little ornaments, looking at them and putting them down again in a way that disturbed the balance of their arrangement.

Lindy burned with impatience. But she was made of stern stuff; she would not ask the necessary question. After a while Leonard said casually:

'You are in for a surprise.'

'Why?' breathed Lindy, released at last. 'Is she too dreadful? Oh, dear, I wish Father would realise we are quite grown-up now!'

Leonard continued his tour of the room:

'Everybody's in for a surprise—a whole series of them.' He threw back his head and laughed. 'Father went to meet her himself, you know. She had reduced even him to silence.'

Lindy's already formed picture of a bespectacled gorgon assumed a prodigious magnitude. 'Father will have to get rid of her,' she said indignantly, 'if she's so very terrible.'

'Terrible?' Leonard shot a look at her, and his green eyes glinted. 'Oh, you won't think her terrible. *You* won't,' he added thoughtfully, picking up a Dresden shepherdess from the mantelpiece and turning her over as if looking for her mark of authenticity.

Lindy was about to ask him what he meant when the door opened again and Arran entered. She looked grave and withdrawn, and when Lindy addressed her she started guiltily:

'Oh, there you are, Arran, at last. Where have you been? And where is John?'

Arran murmured an explanation to which, fortunately, Lindy paid little attention. 'Have *you* seen her?' she cried, almost before Arran had finished speaking. 'Leonard has! He says she's terrible.'

'My dear Lindy!' said Leonard to the Dresden shepherdess.

Arran cast a look at him, but said nothing. She crossed over to a chair near the fireplace, where she could sit and watch without being seen. When at last the door was flung open, by a too-violent movement of Ralph's that sent it crashing back against a wall-cabinet, and Mary Dazill entered, nobody stirred or made a move to welcome her in even the conventional way. Arran remained motionless in the background; Lindy, posed at the tea-table, stared haughtily at the intruder, as if some mistake had been made, and this were the wrong house she had entered; Leonard, amazed at the combination of porcelain-like beauty of face with masses of golden curls, when he had expected dark hair severely strained back and parted down the middle, remained poised with one foot on the kerb and still holding the Dresden shepherdess in his two hands. Their father's voice, unexpectedly harsh, roused them:

'Lindy! This is Miss Dazill. Miss Dazill, my elder daughter Lindy. And this is Arran, my younger daughter.' He ignored Leonard and made for the door. 'I shall leave you in their hands, Miss Dazill. They will look after you well.'

He bowed and went. Lindy inclined her head coldly: inwardly she seethed with resentment at the trick which had been played on her. Arran, aware that the newcomer's look, passing over her sister, had sought her out, blushed. Leonard, when his turn came, was unembarrassed. He stepped down from the kerb, and his eyes were dancing with amusement as he placed a chair for Mary Dazill.

She said: 'Thank you,' unsmilingly; and seating herself, folded her small, white, useless-looking hands on her lap. For the rest of the tea-hour they were kept busy trying to find topics of conversation;

all seemed to die at birth, as Mary Dazill looked from one speaker to the other, politely and gravely, and sometimes murmured 'Yes' or 'No.' Even Lindy, always a mistress of tea-table strategy, had to admit herself defeated. First Leonard excused himself and slipped away; then Arran found that she had some watering to do in the garden. Finally, Lindy, realising that she was on the point of a fit of hysterics, made some hasty excuse and went away, forgetting even to ring the bell for the servant to clear away the tea-things.

Mary Dazill sat there for a few minutes. Then, thoughtfully, she herself rose and rang the bell. The maid who entered looked round in surprise, thinking that the room was empty as no one sat at the table. She started when Mary Dazill, without turning, spoke to her:

'Miss Lindy wishes you to clear.'

The maid, astonished, muttered: 'Yes, miss,' but the presence of the small, silent stranger disturbed her, and made her movements awkward. She dropped no less than three things on to the floor. The last of these, a cake, rolled across the carpet to Mary Dazill's feet. But Mary Dazill sat there motionless, as if unseeing, and did not lift a hand from her lap.

All her life afterwards, at intervals, Betsy used to try to explain the strangeness of the feeling that came over her—the terror, the panic, she would have said, if her vocabulary had included these words—the 'funny feeling' which came over her at the thought of crossing the room to where Mary Dazill sat motionless, and picking up the scone which lay touching the hem of her skirt. She managed to do it, somehow; but her listeners gathered that there was something about that small figure—her stillness—the sense she gave you that she was watching you—that made it harder to approach her than it would have been to put one's hand into a lion's cage.

6

Next morning, when the sun shone and the birds sang and a new day, hardly linked to the old one, was born, everyone wondered why he or she had been so—what was it?—emotional, hysterical?—the evening before. When Mary Dazill entered the breakfast-room, she seemed all that a ladies' companion should be: neat, discreet, unobtrusive, herself a perfect lady without a lady's capriciousness or sense of her own importance, which are the products of money and security. Ralph de Boulter, dressed in riding-kit, had just finished his breakfast when she entered; he rose, not so much out of courtesy to her as because it gave him a chance to get away before conversation began; and at this time in the morning, in the full strength of his manhood, and the full glory of his height, breadth, and abounding health, he seemed to dwarf her entirely. He himself could not remember why he had had all those queer thoughts about her yesterday, or those absurd suspicions of his friend Lady Millborn. Obviously dear Augusta had seen Mary Dazill exactly as he saw her now: the right person for the job. He gave her a brief good morning and went away.

Leonard looked in for a few minutes, gave them all a bright smile, drank a cup of coffee and went off again, no one knew where. The three young women were left together; and polite conversation began. This morning Miss Dazill did not seem at all for a loss at words: she asked, with just the right amount of interest, about their usual occupations, their tastes and hobbies, their social activities. She praised the house, the garden, the countryside, even the weather, though in such a way as to show that she knew her opinion to be of no great importance. Lindy, who at first sight of her had drawn together her fine black brows in recollection of her defeat the evening before, began to expand. She felt she had been mistaken last evening; it must have been the confusion of seeing a young and pretty woman when she had expected a woman of the chaperone class, that had so much upset her. Obviously she was a match for this unassuming, well-mannered stranger, who knew her place so exactly. And there was clearly much to be learnt, in poise and ease of manner, if not in more intellectual subjects, from Mary Dazill...

'And so you are engaged to be married,' said Mary, and added reflectively, 'at eighteen.' She let that remark lie for a moment, just long enough to make Lindy wonder if what she was expressing were envy or some sort of doubt. Then she continued: 'And your fiancé—he is much older, I suppose?'

'Oh, no!' said Lindy, laughing at the thought of an elderly John. 'No, he is only two years older. He is still at Oxford. When he comes of age we shall be married.'

'So you still have eighteen months of—girlhood ahead of you,' said Mary, in the same reflective tone. 'It's quite a long engagement. But then, your fiancé is young and impatient... he was anxious to make clear to the whole world that you were his.'

'Oh, yes, of course,' said Lindy, somewhat confused. She could not help remembering that actually the engagement had been pressed on by John's people, who were anxious to ensure their son's share in the de Boulter fortune. Her father had resisted the idea: he regarded John Despenser without any great enthusiasm, and he wanted Lindy to wait and look around her before choosing. But Lindy, carried away by first love, had overridden all his objections. She had not stopped to ask herself whether, if she had not taken such a strong line, John would have done so. She had assumed that it was her part to persuade her own father. It was not until this very minute that she saw quite clearly how as a matter of fact John had had very little to do with it all.

She turned to look at Mary Dazill almost with apprehension: what a devilish gift the little creature had for undermining one's self-confidence! Was it deliberate? But no, it couldn't be: she had said nothing, nothing at all. She had turned now to speak to Arran:

'And Miss Arran—is she still fancy-free?'

Arran blushed to the roots of her hair. She was fair-complexioned, and blushed easily; but the blush was so deep and so complete as to be embarrassing even to the onlooker.

'Oh, yes,' she stammered. 'I—I—'

Lindy came to her rescue. 'Arran is only seventeen,' she said coldly. 'She has hardly had time to meet anybody. We have only just left school. John is my brother's friend,' she added, as if to explain why, if Arran had had no chance to 'meet' somebody, she, Lindy, had been more fortunate.

'Seventeen,' murmured Mary Dazill.

'Personally,' went on Lindy dogmatically, 'I don't think Arran is likely to marry young. She will be *at least* twenty-five, I think, before she marries. She is much younger for her age than I was, and it will take her longer to grow up.'

Mary Dazill said nothing. She merely looked at Arran. Arran, having blushed till she could blush no more, sat in acute discomfort, looking down at her fingers as they twisted a small handkerchief round and round.

'Well,' said Mary Dazill at last, 'if you have finished breakfast I think we should start work. Your father says we may use the library for our studies in the mornings. I had a talk with him last night...'

*

For the next two hours Lindy and Arran had the painful experience of finding out that they were, by the standards of civilised society, quite uneducated; and worse still—for they had never suspected it—that this mattered. Their girls' school on the South Coast had been very expensive: they had learnt to ride well, to dance, to play the piano and sing, to execute every possible sort of embroidery— though of course not to do any useful sewing, beyond hemming, gathering and smocking. Languages—French and German were also part of the curriculum; but they soon found that they had been misled in thinking that they knew anything of these tongues. For two hours Mary Dazill made them read to her in turn passages from *Eugénie Grandet*; and at every line, almost every word, she quickly corrected their reading until she had reduced both of them to a state not very far from collapse. Lindy came out of the ordeal better than Arran; surprisingly, she kept her temper while Mary Dazill corrected blunder after blunder. She plunged on as if determined that her tormentor should not have the satisfaction of seeing her efforts succeed; but her eyes burned, and her head ached, and she knew that her afternoon's shopping with John's mother was ruined in advance. Arran, after one or two displays of temper quite unusual to her, suddenly felt tears pricking at the back of her eyes and asked to be excused.

'No, no,' said Mary Dazill, looking at the little enamelled watch pinned to her bosom. 'I've been inconsiderate. You must forgive me.' She put her book aside, and went over to Arran and laid a hand on her shoulder. 'I had no idea you were so—sensitive!'

Arran, of course, promptly burst into open weeping and was forced to rush out of the room.

'Well!' said Mary Dazill, gazing after her as if in dismay, 'what a bad teacher I am! You *must* forgive me—I have had so little experience—I had no idea these things could be so tiring.' But her look expressed the thought: 'How queer to be so ignorant, a great girl like that!'

Lindy regarded her coldly.

'You must excuse *us*,' she said. 'We are inexperienced too. We have lived very sheltered lives. We haven't travelled about at all, like you.'

The two young women met each other's look directly for the first time; and it was like the crossing of swords before the duel.

Arran, lying on her bed, was weeping. It was not really the exposure of her ignorance, nor the nervous exhaustion brought on by being continually checked that made her cry like this: she would never have made such an exhibition of herself down there, if it had not been for the thing that was devouring her heart—her passion for John.

If only he had gone on ignoring her, as he did when first Leonard brought him to the house! At first, he had taken less notice of her than of the dogs and the horses, though he was always polite. And she had hardly given him a serious thought, either. At first he had been simply Leonard's friend; then, as time went on and it became clear that he was interested in Lindy, she, Arran, had placidly accepted him as her future brother-in-law. She knew that this label would one day attach itself to a real man, with a face, a shape, a name; John slipped into the vacant position quite easily. And so, just because she found it so easy to accept him, she was off her guard: she was seeing him, often daily, watching him, his way of walking, standing, riding, giving Lindy his hand. She was hearing his laughter, watching his smile, which began, more and more, to alight on *her*. Yes, John began to notice her, greet her—after Lindy, of course, and the others—and finally, look out for her eagerly...

It had all happened so imperceptibly! He took to putting a hand on *her* shoulder as well as Lindy's, when they stood side by side and he came up behind them. In the eagerness of conversation, he would take Arran's arm, or even her hand—in front of Lindy, just like a brother. She, Arran, had accepted all this, because it was done so openly and naturally. How could one be afraid of somebody who laughed so much? And yet, when she looked back, she wondered if she hadn't, really, known all along, and refused to see it, because to see would have meant putting an end to it—and she could not bear to do that. She could not bear to look forward to the days when John would no longer be there, lying in wait for her, watching her... Oh, she could bear his absence—provided he thought about *her*, above everything and everybody! But his presence, when once all this sweet and dangerous by-play was ended—as it must be very soon now—that was what made the days ahead seem intolerable.

There was another reason, beside the obvious one—loyalty to Lindy—why it must cease: and that was Mary Dazill.

At the thought of the newcomer, a cold fear struck through Arran. She did not know why; but some inner perceptiveness told her that Mary Dazill's coming menaced the happiness of all three of them, unless she, Arran, withdrew quickly and left the field to Lindy and a conventional solution. There was no time, now, for dallying or finesse, or allowing oneself to taste for a few days longer the fruits of a forbidden paradise, even in thought. Mary Dazill was quicker than thought. Already, Arran was convinced, the little creature had seen right through her—and she, like a fool, had betrayed herself with her nervousness, her blushes and tears!

One thing only was clear to her: she must see John, and explain to him the danger. *He* was not serious: she knew that. He still intended to do as everybody wished, and marry Lindy; perhaps he wished it himself, in so far as he wished to marry at all. It was just that he had been unable to help collecting Arran as well, on the way. But he would see that this could not go on, now. She was willing, for her part, to sacrifice her pride and let him know the full extent of his conquest, if only that would satisfy him and make him go away. She *must* make him understand—something that threatened—some danger. This time, he must not laugh—for the danger threatened all of them, him as well.

If only she had the courage to warn Lindy too! But no, that she could not do. Lindy was too proud—not quick to suspect treachery, but absolutely intolerant of it. She must be kept out of this, at all costs.

Arran's tears were no longer flowing, now. Her cheeks and eyes burned, but they were dry. For it was no longer of John she was thinking, and her own broken heart, but of Mary Dazill.

'Oh, God!' she thought, 'if only You'd take her away, or make her die!'

It never struck her that her prayer was wicked or blasphemous: it seemed to her the only solution.

John paced up and down the rose garden. The neat beds, outlined with grass borders, gave no hint, yet, of their summer glory. The rose-trees, pruned by a good gardener, showed only their bare thorny stumps and slanting marks of amputation; but the edges, to console the ignorant visitor, nodded with daffodils and narcissi. John noticed none of these things: he was wondering, not if Arran would come—he was sure she would—but whether the game was worth the candle. He was fired by Arran's fresh, young, serious beauty, and still more by the obvious disturbance he was able to arouse in her. But he wanted, nevertheless, to marry Lindy, not only because she would be rich, but because she was by nature masterful, domineering, possessive, and he preferred those qualities: he knew that Lindy, proud and arrogant, adored *him*, and he was sure, too, that she would never let him go. This might be, at times, inconvenient, but it was immensely flattering...

A light step on the gravel made him turn suddenly. As he listened, he thought, 'I knew she'd come,' and he felt a touch of contempt. Then his eyes fell on the newcomer. He saw, not Arran, but a young woman, smaller than Arran, yet older: that much was clear from her outline, the way she moved and wore her clothes. She did not appear to have seen him; she stooped, moving along the border of spring flowers, and picking out the stiff, fragrant white narcissi from among the daffodils. He stood where he was, watching her; and her beautiful profile was thus imprinted on his memory for ever, pale against the dark background of close-clipped yew.

As she came nearer, still absorbed in her picking, he was in doubt what to do. He could not slip away, now, for the rose-garden was enclosed by the great yew-hedge, and there was only one entrance; that was what made it the perfect rendezvous. And yet he hesitated to speak to her, in case she was startled. But if he let her come close up to him, and then spoke, she would be even more startled. He gauged the distance between them, and said, with a nervous laugh:

'Good afternoon.'

To his surprise, she did not start, or even look up for a moment. When she did answer, it was in an indifferent murmur: 'Good afternoon.' Then she would have passed him by. But he barred the way:

'You're Miss Dazill, aren't you? My name's Despenser.'

She looked at him, unsmiling and—or was he mistaken?—accusing.

'Yes, I know.' She turned back to the narcissi.

'You know? But I haven't—you haven't' An absurd nervousness afflicted him, something which he never remembered feeling before. Lindy, for all her rages, only made him laugh. But this was something strange, that destroyed his self-confidence, and confused all his thoughts. Yet he was pleased when Mary Dazill looked him full in the face again, her dark-blue eyes full of scorn.

'Yet I do know you, Mr. Despenser. You are Lindy's fiancé—though for the moment it seems to have slipped your memory.'

'Slipped my memory?' John knew that he ought not to tolerate being spoken to like that, by this stranger, a paid companion. But he could do nothing to assert the difference between them.

'Excuse me,' said Mary Dazill. He was forced to step aside and let her pass. He stood and watched her as she moved along the border, still picking narcissi. He was still standing thus when Arran appeared, breathless and frightened-looking, in the gap between the yew-hedges.

'Oh!' said Arran, looking from John to Mary Dazill, and back to John again. She halted uncertainly in the entrance. John did not attempt to join her. But at the sound of Arran's voice, Mary Dazill turned. She gave a last look at John, and taking up her basket, slipped past Arran with a murmured: 'Excuse me.'

Arran ran to John.

'What was *she* doing here?' she whispered, her eyes wide with fear. 'Oh, John, she frightens me!'

But John said coldly: 'Don't be silly, Arran. You're hysterical. Let's walk along the road and meet Lindy.'

Arran turned away, and in a moment she too, defeated and dejected, followed Mary Dazill out through the gap in the yew-hedge.

John, left alone, picked up a long-stemmed narcissus that had fallen from Mary Dazill's basket, and twirled the stiff, intoxicatingly sweet-scented flower under his nose.

7

Mrs. Barratt turned the page.

'So Mary Dazill arrived,' she said, 'and took her place in the household. With her quiet ways, her attention to her duties, her unobtrusiveness, she seemed the perfect companion. In particular, my mother said, she affected a prim style of dress, intended to emphasise her self-effacement; but actually, it was in such contrast to her remarkable beauty that it had quite the opposite effect. She forced them all, in their different ways, to think about her—with love, or hate. And yet she seemed to do nothing that could attract attention.

'In particular, my mother said, it was strange how, after her arrival, the two young men—John and Leonard—seemed to be always coming home, for odd days, for week-ends. Before, they had vanished, at the end of the vacation, to Oxford; and their families saw and heard very little of them till the next vacation. And even then, they were often away for whole days, amusing themselves, no one knew how. John, of course, had become more assiduous after his engagement to Lindy; but Leonard had always been elusive. Certainly no one would have dreamt of expecting either of them to leave Oxford during term-time, and spend a day at home. It wasn't that they were busy—no one expected young men to work at books in those days—but there were so many amusing things to do, when they got together—drinking, getting into debt and so on. It was a great surprise to their families when, several times during the short summer term, they reappeared.

'Once, she said, they arrived by road, having driven a tandem from Oxford, a distance of about forty miles. They had a reason: they had brought with them a new game, rather more exciting than croquet, with which to amuse the girls. They laughed a great deal as they unloaded the large target, and the long, beautifully-made hazelwood bows. It was the latest craze, they explained: archery, or as the classics preferred to call it, toxophily. Nothing would satisfy them but that the target should be set up there and then on the lawn. They showed Lindy and Arran the correct way of standing, holding the bow, aiming, scoring. My mother arrived that afternoon to take tea with the girls, and she, too, was instantly seized and made to learn the new sport.

'The girls were delighted. At first they were awkward, and the arrows flew wide. But soon they learnt—or at least, Lindy did. Lindy was one of those people who do things well, naturally and easily. It wasn't long before she began hitting the target, and getting nearer and nearer the bull's-eye. She looked like a young Diana as she drew back the string till it touched her breast. John took a picture of her. Here it is. You see how well she stands. That was the target, there, between the two beech trees.'

Mrs. Barratt bent over the book, fascinated, before she handed it across to her hearers.

'And did they teach Mary Dazill as well?' said Dr. Fitzbrown.

'Not on that occasion,' said Mrs. Barratt with unexpected definiteness. 'I remember my mother said that Mary Dazill came out while they were all playing; but she refused to take any part, although the young men begged her. She evidently didn't think it seemly. But later on, when the young men had left again on their long drive back to Oxford, and the three young girls had gone indoors to look at a new frock of Lindy's or something of the kind, a strange thing happened: one of them—Arran, I think—looked out of the upstairs window—Lindy's bedroom was in the turret beneath Arran's, and commanded a good view of the garden—and uttered an exclamation. Lindy and my mother went to look. They saw Mary Dazill, standing on the lawn where each of them had stood just now, and taking aim at the target. She did it with perfect ease, as though she had always been used to it; and when she let the arrow fly, it found its mark not so very far from the centre.

'But what amazed them most of all, and made them all three leave the window hastily, without comment, as if they had been caught spying, was—Ralph de Boulter stood beside her, encouraging her. They could not see her face, as she turned to give him the bow; but they saw his face as he received it. They saw his smile, the way he looked down at her, the way he took the bow as if it were something precious because it was she who gave it. And so for the first time they realised the danger—as they thought it—that threatened them all. They thought they knew the full extent of the danger, and in that, of course, they deceived themselves. But naturally, as good daughters, they set themselves to combat it. Oh, my mother had to listen to plenty of confidences, during that time, while late spring merged into summer...'

'There's one thing to be said for it,' remarked Lindy. 'Now that she goes riding with him in the afternoons, we are spared those dreadful walks.'

Lucy Brown, the Vicar's daughter, nodded. The three girls were sitting in the garden, discussing the ever-burning topic. It was a lovely June day, with blue sky and great white clouds, a day on which no one could be unhappy. Lindy and Lucy, who were great friends, sat close together on wicker chairs, Lindy idle, Lucy busy with her embroidery. Arran had spread rugs on the lawn, a little apart, and lay there brooding, chin on hand, while with the other hand she picked off by their heads all the short-stemmed daisies within reach.

Lucy, always a peacemaker, said: 'Perhaps it will all work out for the best.'

At that, Arran looked up. 'How can it?' she said bitterly.

'You mean, she might refuse him?' said Lindy. 'My dear Lucy, there's no chance of it. Why should she? He's a splendid match for her, from every point of view. At one stroke, she gets position, money, a home, protection against the world. In short, she exchanges a very doubtful past for an assured future—like that man in Homer who exchanged a suit of brass armour for a suit of gold!' She laughed scornfully.

Lucy bowed her head over her work. 'But don't you think, with her looks, she might perhaps—I mean, your father *looks* very young, but after all, you and Arran are here to show up the difference in their ages. And she's of very good family, too.'

'But no fortune,' said Lindy. At this period, Lindy took a particular delight in trying to appear very grown-up and worldly, though actually she was a creature of strong affections and impulses.

'No, but—' Lucy persisted, diffident but obstinate, 'I didn't mean that, exactly. I meant that *she* might wish to marry someone nearer her own age.'

'Perhaps,' said Lindy, 'but perhaps, too, the choice doesn't lie with her.'

'In that case,' retorted Lucy gently, 'she might prefer to remain single. I know *I* should.'

Lindy laughed. 'Why, Lucy, you're positively defending her. You look quite angry. You have a red spot on your cheeks. Don't tell me you, too, have been captivated by the paragon! If so, Arran and I are left alone to fight the enemy.'

Lucy folded her work, and rose. 'I must go now. Father will be waiting for his tea.'

Lindy glanced quickly at Arran; but Arran was still gazing at the lawn, and made no move to join in the pacification of Lucy. Lindy laid a hand on Lucy's arm.

'Don't go, Lucy. I mean, don't be annoyed. Put yourself in our place. It's all very well to be kind and Christian, but—can't you see?' She slipped her arm through Lucy's and drew her away: 'It's Arran I'm worried about,' said Lindy, as soon as they were out of hearing. 'She has been so odd lately—I think, ever since we discovered that my father was attracted by Miss Dazill. She takes it so very hard—much harder than I do. And that's quite natural. I shall get married, and be out of it all. It will scarcely affect me. But Arran will have to stay here, and endure it all, until she meets someone who will take her out of it.'

'Well, that's not impossible, is it, dear?' said Lucy. 'You're only eighteen yourself, you know; and—' She stopped, unable to deceive, and yet unwilling even to suggest what was troubling her. She could not say, to Lindy above all people: 'Can't you see that Arran is in love with John? And if I were you, I wouldn't trust *him* too far.'

Arran watched them go.

Their conversations, their frequent discussions of Mary Dazill, exasperated her, and made her want to laugh, to say to them, 'Why are you so blind?' And at the same time, she was crushed with shame, the burning shame of seventeen, to think of her disloyalty to Lindy. For hateful as it was to imagine Mary Dazill as married to her father Arran would not even think the word 'mother', nor even 'stepmother'—hateful as it was to imagine the little creature as mistress of the house, queening it over her and Lindy and even Leonard, she could not escape from the knowledge that it would at least remove one obstacle out of the way of her own hopeless passion. She did not ask that John should say again, as he had done on that spring day under the cedar, 'I love you.' Clearly he hadn't meant it, even then, though he sounded so sincere; for if he had meant it, he could never have changed. No, she didn't ask that—did not want it—could not have borne it; she could hardly bear the memory. But if only she could get back to the old position, when he smiled at her, spoke to her, above all, was constantly aware of her—she would ask nothing more. If it were only Lindy between them—even if Lindy were his wife—she felt that the old position would be possible.

But now—oh, how *could* Lindy be so blind!—John had looks to spare for no one but Mary Dazill, and smiles to spare for no one at all.

8

John and Leonard, having moored their punt under a willow, lay on the bank with their straw hats tilted over their eyes, and watched the blue rippling river water dance past in the sunshine. They were unlike in temperament: John, in spite of his amorous instability, was essentially serious, Leonard as gay and intangible as a fountain. But they were good friends.

'I shouldn't let it worry you,' said Leonard soothingly. 'It'll pass, you know. These things always do.'

'I don't think so,' said John miserably. 'Not this time. And what the devil am I to do if it doesn't? It's not as if I liked drinking, and there's no war on that I could go to, even if I would. Books don't interest me, people don't interest me, and as for amusements—I can't imagine anything more boring.' He sat up and threw a stone into the water. 'And to think I go through all this for a woman with whom I haven't a chance!'

'Oh, I don't know,' said Leonard in his lazy pleasant voice. 'Everyone has a chance, with every woman—several, very often. I mean, if your first approach is wrong, there are other ways—only most fellows are obstinate and won't try them. The trouble with you is, you're too serious. When you're not, you'll succeed.'

'That's true,' murmured John, thinking of Lindy, and still more of Arran. How easy his conquest had been over Arran! He had thought himself serious there, too, in the beginning. Would that be the end, if Mary Dazill responded as Arran had done? No, never. And anyway, he knew she never would. He had not mentioned to Leonard his escapade with Arran: Leonard seemed to regard leniently his offence against Lindy, but he doubted if even Leonard would be so tolerant if he knew the whole truth.

'Shall I prophesy your future?' went on Leonard. 'You will marry—perhaps Lindy, perhaps not. *My* choice for you would be a nice quiet girl like Lucy Brown, who'd dote on you and keep you in order.' He laughed, and his white teeth gleamed. 'You will enter the Church, and be wonderfully hypocritical about your past, if you ever remember it. As for Mary Dazill—you'll look back upon her kindly and pityingly. By then you'll have persuaded yourself *you* gave *her* up—'

John jumped up, as if he had been stung. 'I'm going to propose to her,' he said, 'as soon as I get back.'

Leonard, too, rose, but slowly.

'And Lindy?' he said. There was an edge to his voice, though he spoke as lightly as ever.

'I shall tell her,' said John hotly. 'I shall ask her to release me. It's not my fault. I—I thought I wanted to marry her. She's a splendid girl. I would have been proud of her. But she's too proud to take a man who loves another woman.'

'There's another point you seem to have forgotten,' said Leonard, and there was a glint in his hazel-green eyes. 'You will have to explain not only to Lindy, but to Arran.'

'Arran?' said John feebly, with averted eyes.

'Yes, Arran. I have *two* sisters, you may remember. You've been making love to Arran, too, haven't you? I noticed the way she watched you, the last time we were there. I also noticed how carefully you avoided her.'

John was silent. He was completely at a loss. He had always counted on Leonard's understanding; and now they were facing each other like enemies.

'You don't understand,' he said at last. 'I've told you—I can't help it—I'm in love with Mary Dazill. No one is more sorry than I am myself. As for Arran, I'm very sorry if I misled her—but that was before I saw Mary.'

'How unfortunate!' said Leonard, 'for Arran. However'—his expression of anger suddenly cleared, as if a strong cool breeze had swept a dark cloud from the face of the sun, and he smiled again, and laid a hand on John's shoulder: 'Don't let us quarrel about this. I admit I was angry with you for trifling with Arran. Lindy can look after herself—but Arran—she's only seventeen, and she's capable of wounds that—unlike yours, you know—*really* won't heal.'

John did not quite like this dismissal of his *grande passion*; but he was so greatly relieved to find Leonard his old sunny self again, that he overlooked the slur.

'Arran's your favourite,' he said impulsively. He added, suddenly overcome with sentiment: 'She's a lovely girl.'

'She is,' agreed Leonard. 'With all respect to your judgment, she's worth a good many Mary Dazills. But that's not saying much. Oh, don't *you* start getting excited,' he said, as John looked up angrily, 'one of us is enough. *She* at any rate isn't worth our quarrelling over.'

'Why have you such a low opinion of her?' asked John, genuinely surprised.

'I haven't,' said Leonard. 'I don't think of her. She doesn't interest me at all.'

'But she's beautiful—you can't deny that.'

'Yes, in a way—but to me she has neither savour nor salt.'

'Be careful,' said John. 'You'll get caught too—like the rest of us.'

'The rest of us?' It was Leonard's turn to look surprised. 'Why? What do *you* know about the rest of her admirers?'

John cursed himself, inwardly. He had not meant even to hint that, before very long, Leonard might find himself in an entirely new relationship to Mary Dazill. Somehow it had seemed so obvious, with Ralph de Boulter going for daily rides with her—but then, of course, Leonard, having been at home only for odd days, could not have noticed this. He, John, had the information at second hand, from his own family. His mother had thought fit to make a journey to Oxford to tell him this, the latest local gossip; and when he had asked her what it had to do with him she had said: 'My dear, don't you realise? If Ralph de Boulter marries this woman, Lindy may find herself disinherited, or at any rate a good deal less well provided for than we had reason to expect when she became engaged to you.' The news had upset John considerably: first because he realised at once that Mary Dazill would certainly accept Ralph de Boulter; and, second, because he would hate to seem to be deserting Lindy at a moment when her worldly fortune was diminishing. He liked to do whatever he did for romantic reasons only; the worldly reason his mother thought so good was a deterrent. It spoilt everything.

Leonard was still waiting for an answer. It occurred to John to tell him the truth: it was, after all, a friend's duty to warn him, and besides, it was not altogether unpleasant to repay Leonard for some of the things he himself had said, and in the same coin.

'Look here, Leonard,' he said. 'I didn't mean to tell you, but I suppose I ought. Your father——' he hesitated, and had the satisfaction of seeing alarm in Leonard's eyes.

'My father?'

'Your father is——very friendly with Mary Dazill——more than friendly. Everybody knows it——everybody who's there. At least, I suppose Lindy and Arran do. That is to say'——he became more and more confused under Leonard's strange, searching look——'I know nothing about this except what my mother told me. But she's not given to gossip, or inventing things, as you know.'

Leonard nodded. He knew Mrs. Despenser well. She was calculating, hard-headed——but her calculations were not based on idle imaginings.

'She gave it me as her considered opinion,' went on John somewhat pompously, to conceal his embarrassment, 'that your father was——infatuated, I'm afraid was the word she used. She thinks your father intends to marry Mary.'

John expected an outburst. But there was none. Leonard stared at him very hard for a moment; then he shrugged his shoulders and turned away:

'Does she really?' he said indifferently. 'Well, don't let that trouble you—or her. There are ways of preventing that.'

He spoke lightly, and John had no idea what he meant. But the remark stuck in his mind, waiting to be explained, and later he was to remember it all too clearly. At present he was sure of nothing except the dull conviction that he had lost Leonard's liking and respect, for nothing at all; since Mary Dazill, even if she were prevented from marrying Ralph de Boulter, would certainly not be for him. Something, he could not tell what, in Leonard's tone, brought that home to him, with chilling certainty.

They turned and went down to the boat, breaking off, by mutual consent, the too-portentous conversation.

'I have an idea,' said Leonard, in his old careless tones. 'When we go home this time, let's take back a set of lawn tennis racquets and a net. The girls could learn to play it: it would amuse them. They must be tired of archery by now—and we shall want some other game as well. When we got bored with them, you and I could play. I'll write a letter and explain about the lawn.'

By the time that they were punting homeward, upstream, it was as if their passage-of-arms and their revelations had been forgotten or had never occurred.

9

'Mary,' said Ralph de Boulter, and his rich, strong voice shook a little, 'will you marry me?'

They were leaning against a five-barred gate at the end of a long avenue of elms down which they had been riding, as they did every morning now, before breakfast.

'It seems early to speak, I know,' he went on, as she did not answer, 'early in the morning and early in our—acquaintance. But I think we know each other well.'

Mary Dazill looked up at him. 'Do we?' she said.

Her tone was quiet, unalarming; it gave him no more than the pleasant, because slight, shock of surprise he had learnt to expect from her.

'Yes, I think so,' he said stubbornly. 'It goes without saying, you know all about me. I've told you all I could, that it was necessary for you to hear. The rest—well, it's merely a question of time. As for you—well, I know all I want to know—I know what you're like—and that I love you.'

Mary Dazill arched the pliable riding-crop between her two small gloved hands.

'But have you thought?' she said.

'About what?'

'About the effect of this—on your family, your children. Lindy and Arran won't take to the idea very kindly.'

Ralph stuck out his strong jaw. 'Lindy and Arran will have to accept my decision,' he said. 'They will have no cause for complaint. I shall, of course, provide for them, and for any children they may have, as I would do in any case—though perhaps not quite so lavishly. But to be fair, I think you're mistaken, Mary; I don't think either of the girls would dream of questioning my choice, in any matter. Why should they? Lindy will soon be leaving home, and surely Arran won't have to wait very long, either. They're very fine girls, both of them; I'm very fond of them and proud of them, too. But I'm not an old man yet; my life isn't over, just because I happen to be a father. By the way, you didn't mention Leonard. I gather you think he won't be so likely to—er—cavil at the idea as the girls will?'

'Leonard,' repeated Mary Dazill, almost to herself. She was thinking to herself:' What a *chef-d'œuvre* of masculine blindness!' but the look she gave de Boulter was admiring as well as pitying, for she was well aware of his splendid qualities—forcefulness, strength of mind, frankness, and when he chose, kindness. 'Oh; I wouldn't go so far as to say that, Ralph. It may be that Leonard will object most of all.' She smiled, but this time towards the ground.

'Why?' Ralph was genuinely astonished. 'Oh, I suppose you mean because he's my son and heir.'

'Your *only* son,' amended Mary, in a low voice that sent a thrill through de Boulter's frame. So she had envisaged the possibility—the probability—of children. The thought moved him deeply: he could not have spoken what he felt, except that his love for this woman was something quite unlike anything he had ever experienced. Yet he had thought he knew the heights and depths of love. Obscurely he was aware that this time he was in the grip of something more powerful than himself—a compulsion not without its danger. *Was* it the sense of danger that predominated—that attracted him so irresistibly? In a flash he saw for a moment quite clearly that Mary Dazill was right: that his children had everything to fear from this new plan of his, for he would no longer be their protector, once he was married to her. Already they had receded in his mind, from their position of first importance; they had become a little vague, and he tended to forget them in making his plans. They belonged, not to the future after which he strained so ardently, but to the past—and whereas the future always beckons with promise, the past always holds a reproach...

'Leonard must make his own way in the world,' he said sententiously. 'He is lucky to have his father to help him—and that I shan't fail to do. As a matter of fact, Mary, I'm more worried about him than about the girls. He seems so vague—lacking in purpose. I believe he hasn't the slightest idea what he wants to do with his life.'

'Perhaps he wants merely to enjoy it,' said Mary.

Ralph looked shocked. 'That's not enough. One must have a purpose. Most youths of his age want to *do* something—or at least *be* something. The other day I was talking to a man who was complaining that his son wanted to be an actor. Well, upon my soul, at least it's something. But Leonard is content just to drift—and as you say, enjoy life. If I had had his outlook, he wouldn't be able to.'

He squared his shoulders, seeing himself once again as the young pioneer. 'I can't understand him,' he added regretfully.

'Don't try to,' said Mary Dazill. 'And don't trouble about him. He will get through life very happily, if he is spared. You see, he has a great asset—he has charm.'

De Boulter nodded. 'Yes, I can see that. Don't think I grudge him his youth, Mary. It's not that. I might, perhaps, if I were less fortunate myself.' He bent on her a smile of trust and happiness. 'But I wish there were a little more—communication between us. Of course, I've seen almost nothing of the lad all these years. I can't expect him to accept me all at once. I may be his father, but I'm a complete stranger, too. The girls didn't seem to mind that—but girls are different.' He interrupted his ruminations to ask her suddenly: 'What did you mean by "if he is spared"?'

Mary Dazill moved away from the gate towards the fencing where their horses were tethered.

'It is just an expression,' she said evasively.

'Not with you, Mary.' He followed her urgently. 'I've never heard you use a superfluous word, or seen you make an unnecessary gesture.' He laid a hand on her arm. 'Tell me what you meant. There's nothing wrong with his health, is there?—nothing I haven't been told?'

Mary Dazill smiled. 'If there is, I know nothing of it. Don't be alarmed, Ralph: your children don't confide in me either. I merely meant that Leonard seems to me to have most of the gifts—but not the instinct of self-preservation.'

Ralph took both her hands. 'What long words my little governess uses!' He laughed, throwing back his head, and did not notice the look she gave him. 'You surely don't mean to say you think he's reckless? Why, he doesn't know the meaning of danger.'

'Exactly,' said Mary Dazill, turning away.

Ralph looked after her, puzzled. Then he shook his head, as if to dismiss these over-complicated analyses, and caught up with her again.

'Then I'm accepted, Mary?' he said.

'Yes,' said Mary Dazill.

He did not dare to ask her if she loved him. For the moment, this was enough.

I O

'I now come,' said Mrs. Barratt, 'to the first tragedy.' By now she was aware that she held her audience. She looked round at the four men—her husband, Mallett, Jones and Fitzbrown—as if they were four schoolboys gathered round her to hear an adventure story. Fitzbrown was the most eager. Her husband, having heard the story before, nevertheless hung on her words, ready to prompt her if she failed anywhere. Mallett, comfortably filling the arm-chair with his huge bulk, pulled at his pipe and stared at the fire, as if seeing there the successive scenes she was describing. Jones, though sceptical, was attending, which was all one could ask.

'You know the situation: Ralph de Boulter was in love with Mary Dazill, and she, for some reason still unknown to them all, had agreed to marry him. It was natural that the three children should dislike the arrangement, even oppose it: children of a first marriage usually do. But Ralph was an ill man to cross; and both the girls, though they talked about it to each other endlessly, and to my mother, didn't dare to show what they felt either to Ralph or to Mary Dazill. The really astonishing behaviour came from Leonard.

'My mother happened to be spending the week-end with the girls when Ralph de Boulter announced his engagement. She has described the scene to me many times. It seems that, being a little in love with Leonard herself in those days, she noticed his every movement. She was prepared, therefore, for his outburst when it came, though the others were not. But even she was not prepared for what happened after...'

It was a July evening, some weeks later, when Ralph de Boulter announced his engagement. He chose an evening when all were present, Leonard and John, Lindy and Arran, Lucy Brown. The evening was warm; and they had dined with the long windows thrown open; they could see the lawn and the trees beyond it, where the ground fell away to the stream. Dusk was falling; candles had been brought in during the meal, and that made the shadows suddenly darken outside; the sky, apple-green at first, deepened to indigo, and occasionally there was a flash of summer lightning on the horizon in the direction of the sea.

Inside the room all was gaiety; the meal was more elaborate than usual to celebrate the home-coming of John and Leonard, and Ralph had ordered wine to be served with each course. He was, in fact, in great good-humour; but the young people did not notice any change in him, partly because he was always pleasant enough, so far as they had ever had the chance to observe; but chiefly because they were engrossed in their own secret longings and antagonisms. Mary Dazill alone sat silent, unsmiling, eating little; the only remarks addressed to her came from Ralph, and these she answered as briefly as possible, looking up quickly and down again. But she looked extremely beautiful. Hers was always the beauty of stillness, irreconcilability; her profile was as flawless as a down-bent face cut in low relief on a marble funeral stele; but her cheeks, usually pale as magnolia petals, had to-night a faint pink flush, and her black eyelashes, as she gazed downward, seemed to lie motionless as though she were asleep. Yet when she did look up, her eyes flashed darkly for a moment before they were hidden again. Her presence seemed to draw the five young people together. Even John, to-night, was ignoring her. He had drunk too much before the end of the meal, and was almost openly trying to hurt Arran by paying renewed and exaggerated court to Lindy. Leonard, a little detached, watched these three; and Lucy Brown, even more outside it all, watched him. Occasionally she spared a glance for Ralph and Mary Dazill; she saw Ralph's reckless assumption of success and happiness; and once she caught a look which Mary, thinking herself unobserved, cast in the direction of the younger group. Lucy thought, though she was not sure, that this look, darting like a serpent, was aimed at Leonard, who leaned back smiling, his fingers on the base of his wine-glass.

At last it was time for dessert. Lindy, glancing at her father, would have risen and given the signal to the other three women; but her father checked her.

'Not yet, Lindy. I have something to say to you all.' His rich voice had a tremor in it; but its loudness made them all turn. He rose, rather slowly and portentously:

'I am obliged, for obvious reasons, to make this announcement myself. But I hope I shan't also have to ask you to drink to our happiness.'

Four startled faces now gazed up at him. Lucy alone still watched Leonard. She saw the smile die on his face; and she saw, but could not interpret, the look that replaced it. The pity for him, and the fear that shot through her then was a physical pain about her heart. She took care to move a little, so that her own face was in shadow.

There was a moment's stillness. The scent of roses, and something even sweeter—honeysuckle, perhaps, or jasmine, or both— floated in through the long windows; the flames of the candles bent away for a second, and then straightened themselves.

'I have to announce,' went on Ralph de Boulter, 'my engagement to be married. I have succeeded in obtaining the consent of Mary—Mary Dazill.'

He held out his hand towards her. Mary Dazill rose, touched his hand, and let her own fall to her side again. She did not join him at the end of the table. She stood in her own place, still looking down, still unsmiling.

This time, the silence lasted longer. It was Leonard who broke it. He thrust back his chair, and rose, glass in hand. John, pale and agitated, slowly imitated him. John was much taller than Leonard, but he stooped now and leaned forward with one hand on the table. Leonard, erect and smiling, looked round:

'Well,' he said with cheerful insolence, 'this *is* a pleasant task. I won't pretend it's a surprise—we've all been more or less prepared for it, haven't we?' He smiled round at his own little circle: Lindy, already slightly puzzled by his manner, frowning, Arran only half listening, thinking her own thoughts still, Lucy Brown anxious and alarmed, John full of self-pity, though his head was swimming and he was not quite sure what was the latest reason for his sorrow.

'But I'm delighted,' went on Leonard, looking down for a moment—for he did not yet care to glance towards his father and Mary Dazill—'that it falls to me, as the son of the house, to express the feelings of you all.'

At this, his smile broadened, and his tone became so obviously a caricature that it penetrated even to Ralph's thickly-armoured consciousness; his look of pride faded, his nostrils widened and his brow twitched with the beginning of a frown. But the frown was one of awakened attention merely—not yet of anger.

'The feelings of you all,' repeated Leonard, charmed with his phrase. He held up his glass, and gazed at it as if fascinated by the glowing ruby of light in it. 'And my feelings, too—mine above all. I wish you joy of the new—arrangement. Come on, girls, you must drink this toast as well. To the happy pair!'

Lindy and Arran rose; Lucy watched in the background. The two sisters, their eyes fixed on Leonard, seemed hypnotised into copying him. But Lucy did not drink the toast. She did not even stand while the others drank it. Leonard drained his glass, Lindy and Arran touched theirs with their lips.

'Of course,' went on Leonard, 'we haven't known Mary—I may call you that, mayn't I?' he said, glancing at last towards her. Mary

Dazill had sat down when the others rose; and now she was, as before, staring down at her hands folded on her lap. It was Ralph, not she, who shot a look of rage at Leonard. 'We haven't known Mary very long; but then, we haven't known our father for long, either—so that everything evens out as it were, doesn't it?' He laughed softly. 'I mean, things that are equal to the same thing are equal to one another, aren't they?—and so they, too, scarcely know each other, and it ought all to be *most* romantic.'

By now, everyone at Leonard's end of the table was frankly terrified. Arran's eyes had opened wide. Lindy, less easily daunted, nevertheless gripped the table, and cast a forlorn look at John. But John had sunk back into his chair, and was gazing at the floor, as if he hoped for escape there. Yet the most frightened of them all was Lucy, since she was frightened for Leonard only.

Ralph de Boulter got up, flustered and still uncertain what to do, though he was certain now that he as well as Mary was being insulted. He could not believe it possible that this young lad, as he thought him, unformed still in body and mind, should dare to stand in front of him, his own father, and poke fun at him, with picador-like insolence. A slight gesture from Mary Dazill helped to check and confuse him. Before he could think of anything effective to do or say, Leonard had set down his glass, and come quickly round the table to where Mary Dazill was sitting. He put his hands on her shoulders:

'And now, I think I'm entitled to kiss the future bride,' he said, and stooping down quickly, he kissed Mary Dazill on the lips.

'Good night, Mary. Good night, Father,' he said, and walked out of the room. The flames of the candles followed him, and recoiled again as the door closed gently behind him.

I I

They all sat in amazed silence, for a few moments after Leonard had gone. Ralph de Boulter was the first to recover speech.

'Mary,' he said, with an effort, 'will you please go with the others to the drawing-room? I shall join you presently.'

He got up. His rage made him incapable of further words, but his gesture made it clear to Lindy that for the first time he expected her to give place to Mary Dazill, in all matters of precedence. He held the door open for Mary; but he had not the patience to wait any longer. Lindy and Arran, following him, saw him cross the tessellated hall, towards the library; and as they moved, escorted by John, towards the drawing-room, they heard voices, their father's and then Leonard's:

'Where are you going? I wish to speak to you.' Their father's voice was thick and barely controlled.

'Oh, certainly.' Leonard's voice was nonchalant, as usual. He had been coming out of the library with a book, on the way up to his room, when he was intercepted by his father. His tone expressed, even in those two words, his view that all this was very tiresome, but he supposed it must be gone through. He turned, and the two went back into the library. The heavy curtained door closed behind them, and the girls heard no more.

It was Leonard who turned up the wicks of the two wrought-iron standard lamps, carefully as if the exact degree of light were important, and Ralph who fumed meanwhile, waiting to get his attention. Leonard drew the heavy dark red curtains across the windows, with a rattle of their big wooden rings on the pole, before he turned with his tantalising air of considerateness, that of a younger man to an elder man, back to his father.

'Well, sir?' he said lightly. 'What is it? I hope I haven't said or done anything to spoil the occasion.'

He came nearer, as if daring Ralph to act upon his rage and knock him down; and beside Ralph's broad-shouldered, powerful frame he looked absurdly slim and youthful. But he had the spiritual mastery, and Ralph de Boulter could not quite meet his eyes.

'You have chosen,' muttered Ralph, 'to be insolent to me at my own table—and worse still, to the woman I intend to marry. If that is how you feel about it, may I ask you to leave this house? I am sorry to have to say such a thing to you. You are my only son, after all, although we scarcely know each other. But you leave me no choice.'

Leonard listened, his head on one side: he was still faintly smiling.

'You'd really turn me out of the house?' he said.

'I—I didn't say that,' said Ralph de Boulter irritably. 'I asked you to go, if you felt that you couldn't be civil to Mary and myself. You must see for yourself, I can't have that. Nothing was farther from my mind a quarter of an hour ago. If you give me your word of honour that that sort of thing won't occur again, I will gladly forget it. I realise, it must be a shock to you—to all of you—at first. But you seem to forget, my life isn't over. I—' He seemed suddenly to realise that he was getting dangerously near explaining himself and even apologising; he pulled himself up with a jerk. 'However, if you can't act like a gentleman, you'll have to go. I shall continue your allowance, of course. I've no wish to be vindictive. It's just that I cannot have you criticising my actions.'

Leonard thought for a moment. 'And do you really mean to say,' he said, 'you would forbid me this house, for the sake of that woman?'

'Stop!' shouted Ralph, beside himself with renewed rage. He raised his hand, not to strike Leonard but to make him stop speaking. 'I see you're incorrigible. You're determined to defy me. Well then, go. I have no more to say to you. Go at once. Or if you can't get a train to-night, you must go by the first train in the morning.'

Leonard gazed at him. His smile faded, and an expression of intense seriousness crossed his face. Ralph had expected him to give up the discussion immediately, and go; he was astonished when Leonard turned away, and sat down in one of the big leather arm-chairs.

'Sit down, please, Father,' he said, waving his hand towards the other chair. 'I want to talk to you seriously. At least, I want to try. I don't know if it's possible.'

Ralph stared down at him uncertainly. He wondered why this sort of thing, the reverse of everything he knew by experience and by hearsay, should happen to him. Here, apparently, was his own son, a youth not yet legally of age, preparing to 'speak seriously' to him, his father! This boy had never seen anything of life except the inside of school and university; Ralph had crossed half the world. Yet the elder, the man of experience, was to listen to the untried youngster! That he was Leonard's father perhaps counted for less: he admitted that; for it was true they hardly knew each other. But—

Nevertheless, Ralph sat down.

'Listen, Father,' said Leonard quietly. 'I want to say to you one or two things that aren't usually said by sons to their fathers. I couldn't do it if I'd known you all my life as a father. It's because, to me, you're almost a stranger, I can. It's a very odd relationship, yours and mine, you know. I call you "Father" out of politeness; but since I've never had a father, naturally I've never felt the need of one—and I can't begin now. So please forget I'm your son, and just listen.'

He spoke so earnestly that Ralph was disarmed. Besides, there was reason in what he was saying. One could not, he was bound to admit, descend from abroad upon these young people and hope to be accepted as the all-wise and all-powerful ruler of the home. Ralph believed himself to be advanced in his views. Irritation pricked at the back of his mind, but he composed himself to listen further.

'And yet,' Leonard went on, 'although we don't know you, and haven't the slightest influence on your actions, *you* have tremendous power over *us*. You can make or mar *our* futures. You can leave us as you found us—perfectly happy, with our own lives, friends, and the things we like doing and plan to do—or you can smash it all up for us. So you see, it's not surprising if we watch your doings rather anxiously.'

A trace of the old lightness crept into his voice at these last words. Ralph looked up sharply, expecting to see that smile which made him wince and enraged him. But Leonard was still quite serious. There was a long pause. Ralph said at last, stiffly:

'I take it you are referring to my intended marriage. I do not see that that concerns you. In any case, I cannot allow you to interfere—'

Leonard jumped up suddenly. 'I'm telling you,' he said, 'if you marry that woman, you will ruin the happiness of every one of us here—including yourself—'

'What do you mean?' blustered Ralph, taken by surprise. 'How can it possibly—'

'By putting us all in her power,' interrupted Leonard. 'You yourself will be in her power—and whatever you may think now, you won't be able to be reasonable or fair—she won't let you.'

Ralph stood up, shaking with rage again. 'Have you any single fact to put forward in support of these fantastic charges?' he said.

'Not one—nothing but my sure knowledge of that woman's character.'

'You, a judge of character?' Ralph laughed scornfully. Good God, boy, get back to your books and don't presume to talk about character to a man twice your age, who's been round the world and met more men than there are books in your College library! Is this the latest fashion—for children to advise their parents? Am I mad, or are you?'

His scorn left Leonard unmoved. 'All the same,' he said, 'in this matter I'm right and you're not. She has bewitched *you*. Still, if you insist on proof—'

'You *have* proof?' Ralph pounced on him.

'Not yet. But I'll get it for you. No—I'll do better than that. I'll demonstrate to you, here in this house, before your eyes, that Mary Dazill is no fit person to be the second mistress of it.'

'I don't know what you mean,' said Ralph, 'you impudent puppy, nor what you're insinuating. But—either you take that back, or else you get out of here.'

' Then you're afraid,' said Leonard, 'to let me stay here and prove what I say?'

Ralph was speechless.

'It's for your own good, remember,' said Leonard, 'as well as for ours.'

Suddenly, Ralph threw back his head and laughed, almost too heartily. 'I give in,' he said. 'You can stay. I must be getting really middle-aged, if I lose my sense of humour so far as to take you seriously. Yes, stay, my lad, and do your damnedest. I promise you, I won't give your little game away—to Mary. But if you're not too proud to take a little advice from your own father in your turn—even though he's a stranger to you—forget about all this. Reconcile yourself to the idea—it won't mean any change for you and the girls. Take it like a sensible fellow—and so you'll always have a home to come to. You don't understand everything yet, you know.'

He laid a hand on Leonard's shoulder. 'Go and join the others,' he said kindly, 'or if you'd rather not, go to bed and we'll make a fresh start in the morning.'

Leonard waited for a moment, motionless under the weight of the well-meaning hand; then, when politeness allowed, he detached himself carefully, said 'Good night', and went quickly away, leaving Ralph, flushed and uneasy, staring after him.

I 2

It was after this painful scene,' said Mrs. Barratt, 'that an extraordinary change in Leonard took place. I don't mean a change of manner: no, he was if anything more gay and charming than ever, my mother said, and in addition, much more sociable. Before, they had seen very little of him; now, he seemed to be always there, with the family; and if any of the others tried to wander off, he would stop them or fetch them back, as if he wanted the party to keep together and not break up. It must have been rather trying for some of them—John, for instance.

'But to come back to the change in Leonard himself. It was the last thing anyone expected: he began to pay assiduous court to Mary Dazill.'

Mary Dazill was walking down by the river when Leonard caught up with her. It was morning; the sun was shining, and there was a scent of wild thyme and peppermint blown across from the island in mid-stream opposite. Mary Dazill walked every morning, now, along this path which ran under the firs, so close to the river that the roots of the trees jutted out over it, through the rich black soil of the bank. Since her engagement to Ralph, she no longer troubled to read with Lindisfarne and Arran in the mornings. It was well known that she liked to have this time to herself; even Ralph never attempted to follow her, but went off on horseback on business connected with his estate.

When she heard footsteps, she turned as if at bay. Leonard came up, laughing.

'I've been wondering where you escaped to every morning,' he said. 'Is this your favourite walk?'

She did not answer, but resumed her walking, and Leonard took his place beside her.

'It used to be mine, when I was a little boy,' he said, undaunted by her silence. 'My father and mother lived here for the first few years, you know, before they went to Burma. Lindy and Arran were born here—and I—well, I don't remember any other home.'

'You love it a great deal, I suppose, then?' said Mary. Her voice was low and musical; one noticed it because she spoke so seldom.

'Oh, I don't go so far as that,' said Leonard carelessly. 'I'm not attached to places. I've been uprooted too often to fall into *that* mistake. And in any case, I like to move. I want to travel. A home means very little to me at present.'

'You are fortunate,' murmured Mary Dazill.

'Why? Oh, you mean *you* set great store by a home.' He laughed. 'I understand that very well, but that's because you're a woman. My sisters feel the same as you, I dare say.'

He cast a sidelong look at her, to see if this shaft went to its mark, and was pleased to see her bite her lips. Her answer startled him:

'Then I am afraid they will hate me more than ever, when the time comes for them to leave here.'

'You mean,' said Leonard, 'when you and my father get married?'

She looked up at him. 'I'm afraid I shall not be able to share my home with them—or you.' She looked extremely beautiful as she said this: they stood in the path, facing each other, Mary Dazill angry and brooding, Leonard laughing and undisturbed.

'With me?' he said. He put his two hands on her shoulders and looked down into her dark blue eyes. 'I haven't asked you to share your home, or anything else, with me, Mary. Not yet, that is.' And he bent and kissed her, for the second time, on the lips.

She did not resist. She remained looking at him, no longer angry, but dazed, almost hypnotised. Her lips were parted; and triumphantly he read in her face all he had hoped for. But he did not kiss her again.

'Shall I show you,' he said, 'where I used to play?' He pointed out over the stream. 'You see that little island?'

Mary Dazill looked.

'We called it Butterfly Island,' he said. 'In winter, when the river rises, the water rushes past, and you couldn't get near it, even in a boat. Sometimes it's quite covered. One could easily drown. But now you can cross to it without getting your feet wet, if you know the way. Follow me, and I'll show you.'

He led the way down the steep crumbling bank by a zigzag path; and Mary Dazill followed, placing each foot where he told her, and letting him steady her with his hand. They came safely down to the river-beach, thick with rounded pebbles; and there across the narrow strait was a line of stones marking a ford to the island. He led her through the tall, waving grasses to the high rock at one end, on which one could sit and watch the waters of the river divide. For a long time she sat there, while he stood at the edge and threw stones into the river; at last he turned and came towards her, smiling. But still he said nothing. He sat at her feet on a shelf of rock and gazed upstream, where the trees dipped their long branches into the ripples.

In the end it was she who spoke first.

'I suppose you are wondering,' she said in a low voice, 'why I am going to marry your father.'

Leonard did not answer for a moment. Then he said: 'You see those trees, hanging out into the river? You'd hardly think, to look at them, would you, that they'd known what it was to be drowned, over their tops in water? And yet it is so. If you look, you can see the grass still tangled high up in their branches.'

'Yes, I see,' said Mary Dazill.

'Yet it all looks very calm and placid now.'

'Yes.'

Leonard turned round to look up at her, smiling. 'That's what will happen to *you*, Mary, when you really fall in love.' '

'You are very sure of yourself,' said Mary Dazill. 'You seem to think you know all about me. Perhaps you can tell me when this devastating event will happen, and—'

'It has happened already,' said Leonard.

Mary Dazill laid one of her small hands on his shoulder. If I thought that,' she said, 'I would shoot myself—or you.'

Leonard gazed up at her, all innocent surprise. 'Why?'

'Because,' she said slowly, 'you are incapable of love. And I'm not. That's my weakness—my only weakness.' She rounded on him fiercely. But his gaze did not waver.

'A weakness which includes all the others, my dear Mary. Well'—he got up and stretched himself—'marry my father, and you will have the home and security you're so set on. But remember you can't have it both ways. Not *afterwards*, anyway. My father is a man of violent passions—and jealousy is one of them. By the way, did you know that your presence here has destroyed my sister Lindy's happiness, too?'

Mary Dazill did not answer. She was watching him and scarcely seemed to know what he said.

'Poor John!' went on Leonard. 'He's terribly in love with you. He's getting thinner every day. You really ought to throw him a kind word sometimes.'

Mary Dazill, aware of the flattery, yet not quite immune, parried it: 'So you think one ought to be kind to people merely because they love one? Would that really be fair to your sister Lindy? I think it would make her even more unhappy than she is.'

'Lindy doesn't know,' said Leonard sharply.

'She doesn't admit she knows,' corrected Mary gently. 'It might be better perhaps if someone opened her eyes.'

'No. Don't do that,' said Leonard.

Mary Dazill, pleased at his obvious alarm, continued softly: 'Of course, she has had warning of his character already, that is, if she had cared to see it.'

'What do you mean?'

'Don't tell me you have missed it, too—you who are so clever at reading other people's minds. I thought John was your closest friend. Did he forget to tell you that before I came he had already been unfaithful to Lindy, in thought if not in deed? Didn't you know that he had been philandering with Arran, and that the poor girl is breaking her heart for him? You blame me for that, too, I suppose?'

'Yes, I know,' said Leonard—he gave a harsh laugh—'though he tried to throw dust in my eyes. But he has found his Nemesis—in you. We all have, it seems.' He took her two hands and drew her towards him. Again she let him, the same dazed, half-hypnotised look on her face. He kissed her, as before. 'If John could see me here with you,' he said, laughing, 'he would spare you the trouble of shooting me. And yet—you will meet me here again to-morrow, in spite of them all.'

13

'And so,' said Mrs. Barratt, 'this new affair, between Mary Dazill and Leonard, sprang up and developed under their eyes. At first, my mother said, they couldn't believe it: they couldn't believe that Leonard would have the audacity to court his father's fiancée openly, or that Mary Dazill would allow it. But Leonard pursued her quite regardless of what anyone thought, and Mary, though she didn't exactly encourage him, took no steps to stop him. Every day he spent more and more time with her: they were always to be seen disappearing in the direction of the river, or walking in the garden, or sitting apart, deep in conversation. And so every day the tension increased: the others all watched, angrily or nervously, but no one dared to interfere.

'One would have expected that the first to speak would have been Leonard's father. He was the one chiefly concerned, and he was not the sort of man to put up tamely with such a blow to his manly dignity. But for some reason he did nothing. It was almost as if he wished to leave the field clear for Leonard, or perhaps to give them both enough rope to hang themselves with. At any rate, he absented himself most days: he went off on long rides round his estate, and didn't reappear till evening. He was present at dinner always; and dinner was a somewhat uneasy affair; but he showed no signs of annoyance. In fact, he treated Mary with all the consideration due to her, and asked no questions. Whether he ever saw her alone, and said anything then, no one knew. After dinner he used often to excuse himself, saying he had letters to write. This was a great relief to them all; for if he joined the young people in the drawing-room, it seemed to be a signal for Leonard to redouble his wooing of Mary.

'One night, my mother said, there was a particularly unpleasant scene. She happened to be spending a few days, as she did now, more often than ever, with Lindy and Arran; and it happened to be one of those evenings when Ralph de Boulter, urged by Lindy, consented to come with them after dinner and listen to some music. John Despenser was there, too, brooding and sullen, watching Mary Dazill and Leonard: he scarcely ever took his eyes off them, nowadays, and he no longer made any attempt to hide his feelings. First, Lindy played while Arran sang; then, as soon as they had finished, Leonard sprang up and insisted on bringing Mary Dazill to the piano. Once he had got her there he leaned on the piano-top, facing her, gazing down at her with undisguised tenderness; and as soon as she would finish one piece he would suggest another.

'The music grew more and more sentimental. It seemed as if Leonard wished to draw a magic circle round himself and her, to flaunt in the faces of the rest of them that they had absolutely no influence within that circle, and that they never could enter it. Mary Dazill, as usual, was passive: she played the pieces he asked for, and once or twice she attempted to escape, but he prevented her always with another request. The atmosphere grew more and more tense: Ralph de Boulter, watching from his corner, said nothing: but his face was set grimly, and he seemed almost to be holding his breath, he was so quiet. Lindy and Arran drew close to each other, as if for support. John, after a little while, muttered some excuse and walked out of the room. My mother withdrew as far as possible into the shadows and listened to the beating of her own heart...'

Mary Dazill half-rose. 'Please, Leonard,' she said, 'let someone else play now.'

Her hands were still on the keyboard. Leonard laid one of his hands on hers. 'Just one more. Play "Robin Adair." You know it's my favourite. You can't leave off without playing "Robin Adair."'

Mary Dazill sat down again, but reluctantly, and played. Again the two of them seemed enclosed by the soft music in a world of their own, though she looked down as if to avoid Leonard's gaze. There was no doubt that the song meant something special to them, that it was being used to convey some message, from him to her. At the end of it, before Leonard had time to raise his eyes, Ralph came across to the piano. His harsh voice cut through the sentimental haze engendered by the song:

'I think, Leonard,' he said, 'this has gone on long enough. Mary, may I have a word with you—alone?'

Mary Dazill rose obediently, and in a moment they were gone. Leonard was left, still looking down at the piano; he leaned over it and touched a note or two with his finger. Lindy and Arran watched him, appalled. None of them seemed to have remembered Lucy Brown, sitting in the shadows. Lindy was the first to speak:

'Oh, Leonard!' she said breathlessly, 'how *can* you? Father will kill you if this goes on!'

Leonard roused himself. 'He would have a perfect right to,' he said quickly, smiling down at the keys. 'I have played him a foul trick, and he has taken it very well.' He spoke almost to himself. 'I wonder what will happen? Will he do the dignified thing and get rid of her; or will he discover that the welfare and peace of the household depends on his getting rid of *me?* Ah, well!' He came and took Mary's place at the piano. 'We shall soon know.' He began playing. 'Go to bed and don't worry about anything. It's all too complicated to explain.'

'But, Leonard——' Lindy would have pressed him for an explanation. Arran checked her. They went out together, leaving him, as they thought, alone.

So Lucy Brown was left with him alone, while he played quietly to himself. She was not herself very musical, and she did not recognise the pieces he was playing, except that they were 'classical,' and one was a passage from a sonatina of Handel's that she had been made to practise when a child. But she recognised that they were utterly different in kind from the music he had been asking Mary Dazill to play. The pieces he had asked for then were all songs and tunes that Lucy knew quite well; and though they were what she liked, too, she had been a little surprised at hearing him ask for them—yes, and a little disappointed as well. Her admiration of Leonard was such that she took it for granted that his taste was superior to hers.

But it did not seem right that she should sit there and listen without his knowing. It was like eavesdropping. Yet how difficult it was to break in on his thoughts! It must be done though. She dreaded the moment when he would start, turn round, see her—the moment of irritation at being interrupted. She was just bracing herself to come out of her shadowy corner when a much more violent interruption occurred. The door suddenly opened, and John burst in.

'Look here,' he said, 'I've been waiting to catch you alone for a long time. You've been avoiding me very carefully, haven't you? But this time you're not going to get away—not till you've heard what I think of you anyway.'

Leonard had glanced up, then down at the piano again. 'There's no need,' he said. 'I know.'

John came nearer. 'Oh, don't pretend you're bored! You listened to me that other time, didn't you, when I told you how I felt about—Mary? You even encouraged me.'

'Did I?' said Leonard.

'Yes, you did! When I said I hadn't a chance with her you implied I might have if I weren't so serious. You were almost advising me how to go about it.'

'My sister's fiancé?' said Leonard. 'That was odd of me.'

'Oh, for God's sake!' said John. 'Why pretend to be such a prig? You're making love to your father's fiancée, aren't you? And I must say, you're making a fine spectacle of yourself, in front of everybody. If you must behave like that, need you do it openly?'

Leonard stood up. 'I understand,' he said. 'You prefer secret philandering.'

John drew back a step, knocking over one of the small chairs. 'If I weren't in your father's house,' he said, 'I'd knock you down.'

Leonard laughed. 'Don't let that restrain you. He won't mind, I'm sure. And anyway, I shan't be here for much longer—so you can satisfy your outraged feelings then, without transgressing the rules of hospitality.'

John said stiffly: 'I'd better go. But I would like you to know that I shall never enter this house again, if I can help it—certainly not if you are here. I shall write to Lindy, and to your father, to-morrow.'

He turned and walked out of the room. Leonard stood staring after him.

It was then that Lucy Brown nerved herself to speak.

'Leonard,' she called out, and her voice sounded faint and tremulous to her own ears. 'Leonard, I'm very sorry—but I've been here the whole time.'

'Why, Lucy!' He turned, surprised but not annoyed. 'I didn't see you. Somehow I thought you'd all gone and I was alone.'

'I know, I know you did!' Lucy was distressed. 'I didn't mean to spy on you. But it was so hard to get away!'

He took her two hands and drew her down on to a settee beside him. His voice was very kind.

'So you overheard that scene between John and me just now. Tell me, Lucy'—he leaned towards her—'did you understand what it was all about?'

'Yes, yes, of course, Leonard,' she said. 'But please don't think about it: it will go no further. I had no right to be here, and I must behave as if I had not been. Please trust me.'

'I do, Lucy,' he said. He was still watching her with an intent, grave expression that surprised her. 'I do trust you. For instance, I know you would never think evil of me, whatever I did, would you?'

Lucy's voice trembled. 'I try never to think evil of anyone,' she said falteringly.

'But you find it hard sometimes to deny the evidence of your senses?'

She looked up at him then, and met his searching gaze. 'I wish you wouldn't,' she said. 'Please don't be offended. I know it's not my business. But—everybody here is terribly unhappy.'

'I know,' said Leonard. 'And do you know whose fault that is?'

She did not answer.

'I'll tell you,' he said. 'The cause of it all is—Mary Dazill.' His voice had gone hard with hatred. 'Since she came, everything has gone wrong. My father—would sell us all, himself included, for her. My friend—is prepared to sacrifice Lindy, and me, to her. Even the servants are bewitched by her. They obey her, not us any longer. As for my sisters—Lindy's proud, Arran's young and sensitive; they're both helpless before her. And she—she's the original vampire, the creature who comes and sucks men's blood, and gives back nothing—nothing!'

His voice broke for a moment.

'But, Leonard,' ventured Lucy timidly, 'if that is what you think, why do you—pay attention to her so openly? No good can come of that, surely, even if you were sincere. But if you are not, then I don't understand it at all.'

'Listen, Lucy.' Leonard gripped her hands more tightly. 'There is one person in this house who can end all this, and only one—myself. I am the only person who can get rid of her—because for some reason, I am the only one who has any power over her. Not over her heart—she has none—but over her feelings.'

'You mean—she is in love with you?'

Leonard nodded. 'As she sees love.'

'Oh, Leonard! And you'll marry her—though you don't love her—though you hate her? You can't, you can't! Oh, please—'

Leonard released her hands. He laughed. 'Oh, no! *I* shan't

marry her. You don't understand. She is in love with me—at the moment—but she wants to *marry* my father.'

'But, Leonard! How dreadful!'

He laughed again. 'Not at all. Mary doesn't want love—not to live on, anyway. She wants security—a home—if you like, a refuge. From what? Ah, I don't know. I know no more about Mary Dazill than the rest of you. She is a clever woman. Love doesn't make her talk—it drives her into a deeper silence. No: Mary intends now, as before, to marry the man who can give her protection—safety. *She* will not be deflected.'

'Then why,' cried out Lucy despairingly, 'why must you quarrel with everybody for no reason at all—simply to prove—'

'You don't understand,' said Leonard again. 'I told my father I'd show him what kind of woman Mary Dazill was. Well, I've done so— in a way. Hasn't she flouted him openly, in front of all of us, for me? And yet—' He jumped up and began walking up and down the room. 'I see now, I've been a fool. She will convince him in five minutes that all he has seen meant nothing—that she was merely humouring a silly boy. And he'll believe it. His vanity is—impenetrable.'

'Leonard,' said Lucy.

He stopped in his pacing. 'Yes?'

'Are you *sure* that's the whole truth? I mean, is it true that you are only pretending in all this?' She stopped, daunted by her temerity; yet something stronger drove her on.

'You mean?' he said.

'Oh, Leonard—are you sure you're not deceiving yourself? I know you began it all in good faith—but are you sure you're not in love with her yourself, now?'

There was a silence. Again, Lucy listened to her own heart-beats. At last, he answered, solemnly and slowly:

'If I thought that, Lucy, I'd shoot myself, without a moment's delay.'

Soon afterwards she left him. She was still troubled; she had the gravest doubts as to the wisdom of what he was doing. But still, she felt calmed: for on the point that mattered most of all to her, he had reassured her: she no longer believed that he was in love with Mary Dazill.

She went to her room, and slept soundly. Next morning, there came a knocking on her door. 'Come in!' she called out cheerfully, expecting to see a maid who would draw the curtains and let in the sunlight. Instead, she saw Lindy.

'Lindy, Lindy, what's the matter?' Lucy sat up in bed.

Lindy came towards her. 'Lucy—don't scream. It's Leonard. He—he's shot himself, in his room. The maid found him this morning. He was sitting at his desk, by the window—and Father's revolver was beside him.

14

'H'm,' said Dr. Jones, 'so Leonard shot himself. Well, it's not remarkable, considering the mess he had got himself into. By the way, I suppose he really *was* in love with this girl, Mary Dazill?'

Fitzbrown cut in quickly. 'No, no, of course he wasn't in love with her. He was outside it all—that's quite clear from Mrs. Barratt's mother's statement.'

'But she wasn't an impartial witness,' said Jones bluntly. 'She was in love with him herself.'

Mrs. Barratt intervened quietly. 'That is the very reason why she would make no mistake, Dr. Jones, if you'll excuse my disagreeing with you. She *saw* Leonard de Boulter, just as he was—and he was no ordinary person. Do you remember, how I told you—she was aware, when the others left him alone, as he thought, how his playing completely changed? I think that that to her was proof of what she knew in other ways—namely, that Leonard was speaking the truth about his courtship of Mary Dazill. Besides, if he had loved her, he would never have flaunted this in the face of his father and his friend. He was not that sort of person.'

'Exactly,' said Fitzbrown. 'And the reason why he shot himself was that he had failed, and he knew it. He had enraged his father, and alienated his best friend, for nothing. Mary Dazill had won, and so—'

Mallett spoke at last from his corner. 'Did anyone check up on it,' he said, 'at the time?'

The Vicar answered: 'There was an inquest. The verdict was "suicide while of unsound mind." It was all hushed up, of course, and the family maintained that he had been overworking; but the story got about that there was a love-affair at the bottom of it. I believe there was a good deal of gossip in the village, and his name was connected with Mary Dazill. Isn't that so, my dear?'

Mrs. Barratt nodded. 'So my mother said. But—what was that you said a moment ago, Superintendent?'

'I said, "Did anyone check up on it at the time?" I meant, was it ascertained beyond all question that he committed suicide?'

Mrs. Barratt gave a gasp. 'How extraordinary that you should say that!'

'Not extraordinary at all,' said Mallett. 'It's the first question we ask, when there's a corpse: could this by any possibility have been due to foul play? Why? Were there any doubts about it at the time?'

'None at all, Superintendent. That is to say, neither the police nor his family had the slightest doubt, nor anyone else, either—except my mother. She maintained to the end of her life that Leonard de Boulter did not shoot himself.'

'What?' said Fitzbrown eagerly. 'She believed he was murdered? Whom did she suspect? Had she any clues?'

The Vicar stirred uneasily, and his leather chair creaked.

'My dear,' he said, 'do you think we ought to prolong the life of what after all is only an unfounded suspicion? Your mother never gave us any valid reason for supposing that she knew anything definite about this business. And she certainly never voiced suspicion of any particular person. Wouldn't it be better—'

His little homily tailed off weakly as Mallett interrupted:

'*Why* did she think he hadn't shot himself? She must have had a reason of some kind.'

'Oh, yes, she had a reason,' answered Mrs. Barratt calmly, 'though it wasn't one that would have satisfied a coroner—or perhaps even you, Mr. Mallett. Her reason was—well, I suppose you'd call it psychological, nowadays.'

'Oh, intuition!' said Dr. Jones scornfully.

'No, not exactly. You see, she had had a long and intimate conversation with him the evening before. Probably she was the last person to talk to him before he—died. And on that occasion she missed nothing—no lightest word of his, no gesture. Her anxiety, together with her—affection—for him made her observation unusually keen. Well, she said that she was *quite sure* that when they parted, that evening, he had no thought of suicide—no thought of death at all. He was quite calm when he left her—almost cheerful.'

'But,' said Jones, 'you said yourself, he mentioned shooting himself, when your mother asked him if he was in love with Mary Dazill.'

'Yes,' said Mrs. Barratt, 'I know. But, however illogical it may seem to you, that to my mother was the very reason why she was sure he wasn't thinking of it. His speaking of it, to her, was a pledge that he would never do such a thing.'

'I'm afraid I don't follow,' said Jones.

'Then I'm afraid I can't make it any clearer,' said Mrs. Barratt, exhibiting for the first time a touch of impatience. Mallett interrupted:

'Oh, come, Bob! Mrs. Barratt's mother was right. When the young man said: "If I thought that were true, I'd shoot myself," he was saying in the most emphatic way he could, that it was false. "I'd shoot myself," was just an expression.'

'I wonder,' murmured Mrs. Barratt.

'You don't agree?' Mallett was surprised.

'Not exactly. I think, you see, if he really had found he was in love with Mary Dazill, he was quite capable of shooting himself. But if he had been, I believe my mother would have known.'

'Do you think he was murdered?' Fitzbrown leaned forward eagerly again.

'My mother thought so,' said Mrs. Barratt. 'That is all I know. And in the light of what followed, it seems possible that she was right.'

There was a pause. Mallett got up. 'Well, I must be getting back to Chode.' The two doctors likewise remembered their engagements. In a very short time they had left behind them the cosy, stuffy vicarage drawing-room, and the strange, musty atmosphere of half a century ago; they were walking down the road towards the railway station, through the November drizzle. As they passed the dark lych-gate, Fitzbrown said:

'What an extraordinary story! Did he really shoot himself, do you think, or was it murder? Somehow, while the good lady was telling it, anything seemed possible, or even probable.'

'Suicide, of course,' said Jones. 'They imagined the rest, she and her mother, between them.'

'What do you think, Mallett?' persisted Fitzbrown.

'I?' said Mallett. 'I'm a detective, not a clairvoyant. There's nothing to go on. Still, there were two men at least—his father and Despenser—who had good motives for wanting to get rid of him. I'll look up the report of the inquest, some time. But the whole thing is lost in the past. No good raking it all up again.'

Dr. Fitzbrown was not listening. He was already planning to go back there, one afternoon as soon as he could get away, and hear the rest of Mrs. Barratt's story.

Book II

I

A week later Dr. Fitzbrown walked into Mrs. Barratt's draw-ing-room. It was a sunny afternoon in early December, very different from the day of his last visit; and he rubbed his hands cheerfully in front of the fire as he waited for her. His excuse for coming? Oh, that was easy: he had brought over—unofficially, of course—a number of preparations for the Vicar's chilblains, which she had mentioned last time.

Mrs. Barratt came in with her welcoming smile. 'Well, this *is* nice of you!' And before he could display his offerings of calcium tablets and salve: 'Now we shall all be able to have tea together.'

Dr. Fitzbrown looked somewhat taken aback. He was shy and unsociable, and the prospect of a Vicarage tea-party terrified him. Mrs. Barratt smiled slyly.

'Didn't you know? Superintendent Mallett and Dr. Jones are here. Yes, they came over to see the Vicar about something connected with the new police-sergeant who is to take poor Mr. Robinson's place. They've been over to the churchyard to look at the grave.'

Fitzbrown nodded slowly. 'I see. Funny I didn't meet them. But perhaps I was in a different part. To be quite frank, I didn't go to see Robinson's grave. I went and had a look at the grave of Mary

Dazill—then I hung around the de Boulters' vault for a while, hoping to catch another glimpse of the two old ladies. But evidently I was too late: the wreath seems to have been changed already.'

Mrs. Barrett nodded. 'When Lindy and Arran fail to change the wreath,' she said, 'we shall know they're dead or dying. The flowers must never be allowed to wither on the tomb. Ah, here comes the others from the study. I'll ring for tea—well, dear, have you settled all your business?'

Superintendent Mallett, red-haired and burly, and Dr. Jones, fat, short and morose-looking, followed the Vicar into the room. Fitzbrown gazed at them reproachfully; and they returned the look with somewhat sheepish grins; for they had left him a couple of hours ago in Chode, and had not mentioned where they were going.

'Hullo, Fitzbrown,' said Mallett heartily. 'What are you doing here? I thought you had a surgery at six on Thursdays.'

'It's my half-day,' said Fitzbrown gruffly. 'What about you, Jones? I thought you were up to your eyes in that tinned food analysis business.'

'Oh,' said Jones, 'there were a couple of complaints here about well-water, so as Mallett happened to be coming along—'

The Vicar gave a dry chuckle.

'The truth is, gentlemen, you've all come to hear the second instalment of my wife's story. For, like a good serial-writer, she broke off right in the middle, and let you know there was more. Sit down, light your pipes and make yourselves at home. Go on, my dear. Tell them the rest. I don't mind telling you, it wasn't poor Robinson's grave got their real attention this afternoon.'

Fitzbrown had already taken his old chair. He leaned forward. 'Yes, go on, Mrs. Barratt. Tell us how Leonard's death affected them—above all, how it affected Mary Dazill.'

Mrs. Barratt glanced at him for a moment, before turning to the tea-table which the maid had placed beside her. 'You are a romantic, Dr. Fitzbrown,' she murmured, but in so low a tone that the others did not hear. 'It's a very dangerous thing to be—especially about the past. The past has a way of trying to come to life again—at our expense, sometimes. Well,' she turned back to the others, 'as I told you before, no one really knows what happened, except perhaps those who were involved at the time; but I'll tell you what my mother told me, as much as I remember. The rest, I suppose, must remain a secret forever.'

'The death of Leonard,' she resumed presently, when all had been served, 'had, of course, a tremendous effect on the household. Actually, there was not one of them who had really known him intimately, or even understood him; and in fact, not one of them—either his father, or his sisters, or even his friend—had ever lived in close contact with him, as in ordinary families. Apart from their childhood days, before Ralph de Boulter had taken his wife abroad, they had spent very little time together: Leonard had gone to his schools, the girls to theirs; and the friendship between Leonard and John was a comparatively recent revival after a break of many years. For the last few years they had been very good friends; but the truth was, there was something about Leonard that eluded intimacy. John had had good reason to realise that though he might confide in Leonard, there were secrets which Leonard had not shared with him.

'And now he had gone, as suddenly and strangely as a sunbeam, which one minute is shining in through a window, and the next minute has vanished, leaving only a lack of it, a sense of chill and shadow where there was brightness before. They all mourned him. His father went about his business silent and morose; Arran and

Lindy, though they kept up a brave show in public, shed tears when they were alone together, and it fell to my mother to forget her own sorrow and comfort theirs. As for Mary Dazill, for a while the sudden blow made them forget about her, or rather, it benumbed them so that they no longer resented her presence.

'Gradually, the confusion of the inquest, and local curiosity, and gossip, and the comings and goings of the people who seem to flock to a house on these occasions—all had died down, leaving a deadly calm, a kind of clarity in which they could see to the full what they had lost. And when this time came, one thing stood out most clearly of all: the extraordinary change that had come over Arran...'

One day Lucy Brown was sitting with Lindy in her room. They never sat in the garden now, though the weather was still warm. It was early September, fine and mild, still summer-like except for the mist on the lawn as dusk fell, and the heavier morning dew. But the garden reminded them too much of Leonard. In the distance, between the two elm trees, the target still stood. No one had bothered to move it; its painted circles, so bright and gay a short while ago, were—dim and faded; one of the feathered arrows still stuck aslant in the centre.

Lucy, as usual, was sewing, but Lindy sat with her hands idle before her.

'Lucy,' she said after a while, 'tell me—have *you* noticed any-thing strange about Arran lately?'

Lucy looked up. 'I've noticed,' she said, 'how she seems to spend less and less time with us. I hardly ever see her these days.'

Lindy leaned forward eagerly. 'That's it! Lucy, I'm very wor-ried about her. She stays more and more in her room. And if I do induce her to come downstairs and sit with the others she doesn't talk, or smile, or sing as she used to—she sits quite motionless and lifeless, staring into space. Nothing seems to rouse her. I wish I knew what to do. I think, if something isn't done for her she will go out of her mind.' She sighed impatiently. 'I *can't* understand it. Naturally, Leonard's death has been a shock to her—as it has to us all. But would you have said that she was so devoted to him? Why, she had scarcely had time to grow as fond of him as that!' Lindy, impulsive and frank as always, could not help speaking her mind.

'I don't think affection necessarily depends on the *time* one has known a person,' demurred Lucy mildly. 'But still—I see what you mean. Of course, he was her brother—but she showed no *particular* interest in him—nothing out of the ordinary, I mean—while he was here. It certainly is strange that she should take it to heart so much more than—you, for instance.'

Lindy nodded. 'I would have said that it would have meant more to almost any of us than to her—John, for instance, or you, Lucy.' Lucy bit her lip, and Lindy stretched out her hand impulsively. 'Forgive me, Lucy—but I knew—or thought I did—how you felt about him. And I had hopes—before he conceived that extraordinary infatuation for—' She glanced round fearfully, and did not utter the ever-present name. 'However—the point is now, what can we do to get her out of this dreadful lethargy? I always thought my influence over her was the strongest thing in her life—I've always tried to be a mother to her, though there's only a year's difference in our ages. But now—she doesn't respond, and she's getting worse. She doesn't even cry, nowadays.'

Lucy sewed on for a while. Then, having made up her mind, she laid aside her sewing. 'Lindy,' she said, 'did it ever occur to you that Arran's trouble started *before* Leonard died? Didn't you ever notice anything wrong with her before?'

Lindy reflected. 'I didn't, at the time. But lately I've been thinking about her so much—and it *does* seem to me that she was rather strange, for quite a long time before, as you say. Yes, she changed; it was some time ago, at the beginning of the summer. To me it seems to coincide with the arrival of Mary Dazill. Everything, everything dates from that day!' Her voice broke; but her black eyes flashed with hatred.

Lucy spoke soothingly. 'Perhaps, Lindy, dear. But do you know what I think? I think it started even before.'

'You do!' Lindy was surprised, even a little curious.

'I *know* it did. I wondered at the time if I should tell you—but it seemed so interfering, and—and there was no reason, then, why you should be told. But now—'

'Lucy! What do you mean?' Lindy was wide-awake now, and practical, ready to cope with the truth, whatever it was. 'If you know anything about Arran that I didn't, I think you should have told me. She's my responsibility, after all, not yours. And even if she confided in you—though I can't believe she would—'

Lucy interrupted. 'She didn't, Lindy, dear. I was merely using my eyes. You forget, I was apart—able to look on impartially. You were so preoccupied with John, you never noticed—'

'John!' The colour sprang up in Lindy's cheeks. Her voice was haughty. 'What do you mean? What has John got to do with it?'

'Oh, Lindy, can't you see? Arran is in love with him. She has been, for months. She has been eating out her heart, in secret. And when you add to that her sense of disloyalty towards you, and now this shock coming as well... John has been avoiding this house a good deal lately, hasn't he? She is pining away because she never sees him—and because even if she did there still would be no answer.'

Lindy's flush had died and she looked pale. There was a silence. Then she said calmly: 'Are you sure?'

Lucy nodded.

'And can you tell me—does John return her affection?' In spite of her self-control there was a trace of bitterness in her tone.

'I can't tell you that, Lindy. But—forgive me—I do think he is to some extent to blame. I mean, I think he played on her feelings once he was aware they existed.'

'Yes,' said Lindy. 'Yes, I suppose you are right. I've been very blind. And yet—it must be my excuse, Lucy—I never thought of watching him—or her. I was too much preoccupied—like the rest of us—with Mary Dazill. I was watching, first her and my father, then her and Leonard. You remember?—We all three talked about them all the time. So I never saw—and yet, now I'm faced with it, I know, I can't deny it. I haven't been really happy for a very long time. But again I believed she—that woman—was the cause of everything, my own uneasiness and restlessness. Well! Now you've told me we can at least put that right.'

'Lindy!' Lucy stood up, appalled. 'What are you going to do?'

Lindy gave a high laugh. 'Oh, nothing very dreadful, Lucy, dear! I'm not going to *force* them together, if that is what you're afraid of. I see you think I'm the clumsiest creature on earth. No: I promise you, all I shall do is, the next time John is here, I shall ask him to go and see her. I shall send him a note, first, asking him to come over. Then I shall arrange that Arry is somewhere—here, for instance— where they can talk together quite without *arrière pensée*, on either side. If anything comes of their talk, however small, I shall see it. I shall know the moment I see him—or her. If it really is as you say—if she is in love with him—there'll be a change in her at last. And if I think he can return her love—why, then I shall release him.'

'But, Lindy!' Lucy was troubled. 'He is your fiancé. You love him yourself. Is it wise of you to sacrifice your own happiness—'

A strange look came over Lindy's face, making her for the moment look much older than her years. 'I shouldn't be doing *that*, Lucy, dear,' she said. 'Haven't you understood me? One can't sacrifice what one no longer possesses, can one? Leave me to work this out in my own way.'

2

Lucy, left alone, wandered along the corridors of the big, half-empty house. John had responded more quickly than they had expected: Lindy's note, sent by the hand of a messenger, had brought him over at once, as if he had been waiting for a summons. And Lindy, filled now with the ardour of self-sacrifice, had conducted him to her own little sitting-room in the round tower, where he was to meet Arran. Both were to be unprepared for the meeting. Lucy, a little alienated by Lindy's scheming, had drifted away.

She met no one. Ever since Leonard's death the house seemed deserted. It had been meant for a bigger family; but somehow, while he was still alive, it had seemed peopled, full of life. Now the inmates seemed to avoid one another; and one had the impression of a house that was furnished, well cared for by unseen hands, but still waiting to be inhabited. She found herself on the landing above the well of the double staircase overlooking the hall. She wondered if she ought to descend and wait for Lindy in the drawing-room; it did not seem correct to be wandering about someone else's house in this way. But no: she had a mind to explore further. She gave in to the impulse and passed on.

She was now in the west wing of the house. Here the main corridor was dimly lighted from a window at the far end. She passed the many closed doors and the dim staircases leading to the second floor. She knew quite well where she was going; and her heart beat faster, with a sense of guilt to which she was unaccustomed, but something drove her on. If one of these doors had opened, and anyone, even a servant, had appeared, she would have screamed out, as if someone had awakened her from a somnambulist's excursion; but the doors remained closed. Behind them, she knew, was furniture covered with dust-sheets; since Leonard's death this wing of the house had been disused.

She hurried on, her feet making no sound on the thick carpet. At last she came to the door. Was it the door? How could she be certain? She had never set foot in this part of the house before. And yet she did know. How often had she not looked up from the garden at this tower, and thought, 'That is Leonard's room. How like him to choose a room so far apart!' She remembered how the two girls, half-laughing, half-serious, had insisted on their father's giving over to them, as their special territory, the whole of the east tower. Lindy was to have the first-floor room as her boudoir, Arran would have the one above, from which one could climb out on to the roof with its low parapet and cap of red tiles. They had spent endless time and care decorating their miniature homes. And Leonard, when he came home, had just as promptly appropriated the other, the west tower: the only difference between their choice was that their rooms were at the occupied end of the house, whereas he, to reach his, had to traverse the whole of the unoccupied wing.

'And that,' thought Lucy, 'is why none of us heard that shot. No one knows when—much less how—he died.'

Her hand was on the latch. She lifted it. Almost to her relief, the door failed to yield. She looked: the key was still in the lock. Well, it was fated that she should enter. She turned the key; the door swung open, and the bright afternoon sunshine streamed in through the uncurtained windows, dazzling her momentarily. She moved across to the window, and looked down.

Below was the terrace that had been weed-grown for many years, and was now newly covered with yellow gravel. From this window it looked near, as if one could jump down on to it without much hurting oneself. To get a sensation of height, one would have to go up the spiral staircase to the next floor, and out on to the roof, from which one could catch a glimpse of the sea above the tree-tops. Here, drawn up in front of the window, was Leonard's desk, just as she had imagined it, and a swivel-chair.

So one must think of him as sitting here, that night, staring out across the lawn—for it had been full moon, as she well remembered—and then stretching out his hand to the revolver. Then—she could imagine him gripping the edge of the desk with his other hand, as he slowly pointed the barrel at his temple... How did one ever steel oneself to the final act, the finger-pressure that blotted out one's life? What could there be in life, in *his* life, so terrible that it outbalanced the need to take such a decision? Was it not extraordinary that in the long history of the world, any human being not in unendurable physical pain could have been found to throw away the many-coloured jewel of life?—'His head fell forward here,' she thought. She had no recollection of hearing the discovery described; yet from stray remarks overheard she had pieced it together. She knew that he had been found in this chair, with his left arm hanging down, almost touching the floor, and the revolver on the floor near his left hand. His head was on his right arm, which was stretched out across the desk. Almost the only question asked at the inquest about the manner of death had been, was he left-handed? Everyone knew that he was. Two shots had been fired from the revolver; but no one could say whether it had been fully loaded when Leonard took it from his father's room. Perhaps Leonard himself had experimented, out of doors somewhere, with the first shot. There was no trace of any other bullet in that small room. Ralph de Boulter had said so. He had taken the trouble to look, it seemed.

Running beneath the window was a wooden seat, and beneath the seat, book-shelves. What did Leonard read? She had often wondered. She stooped down, lifting up one fold of the curtain that protected the shelves from dust. There were papers, old notebooks, a large tome, a lexicon apparently. She could not see the title. She ran a hand down the book's broad spine. Her hand encountered an unevenness. She drew out the volume, using both hands because of its weight... A voice close behind her startled her. 'Are you looking for something, Miss Brown?'

She turned, to see Mary Dazill standing in the doorway.

3

Lucy Brown rose slowly from her stooping posture. She held the heavy book in her hands, and rested its edges on the desk, across which she faced Mary Dazill.

Mary Dazill came toward her. There was something forbidding in her look; but Lucy faced her bravely.

'Thank you,' she said coldly. 'I hope I have not disturbed you. I imagined that this part of the house was unoccupied—now.'

'It is,' said Mary. 'That is why I was surprised to see you making your way here.'

Lucy Brown flushed with anger, and tossed her head. 'I think this house is still open to me as much as to you,' she said. 'When you are mistress of it, believe me, I shall not trouble you. Until then—'

Mary Dazill regarded her for a moment from under bent brows. 'You are insolent,' she said; and then, 'You have more spirit than I thought. Oh, please don't stay behind there. I assure you, I am not dangerous.'

Lucy thought, 'Are you not?' but she did not say it. Instead, she came out slowly, leaving the big book where it lay on the desk. They confronted one another.

'I have been wanting to speak to you for some time,' said Mary. 'I believe you have a considerable influence on—my two charges. Why do you use it against me?'

'Against you?' said Lucy. 'I assure you, I do nothing of the kind. I wouldn't presume to do such a thing in any circumstances.'

'No, of course not,' said Mary Dazill. 'It would be contrary to your code. But you cannot deny you are hostile to me, and you encourage *them* to be hostile, too. You stand between them and me. If it were not for you, I could—' she stopped, and bit her lip, as if ashamed of having momentarily displayed feeling. She turned aside. 'Is it such a crime on my part' she said, 'to want a home of my own and a husband? Need his daughters be quite so stubbornly loyal to their mother? They have never seen her since they were too young to remember her clearly. Need they grudge their father a renewal of his happiness? *They* can't and won't provide for it, you know.'

Lucy was surprised. She had never heard Mary speak more than a few consecutive words before.

'Perhaps you are right,' she said hesitantly, 'in that. I don't suppose Lindy and Arran would have gone on resenting that for ever—though you have done very little to help them to accept the situation, have you? But—why did you let Leonard behave like that towards you? You *must* have been encouraging him—and yet you knew it would make his father furiously angry—you knew poor Leonard had nothing to gain and everything to lose. *That* was what they couldn't forgive you. Oh, why did you do it?' She turned and gazed down at the desk with a gesture of despair: the tears streamed from her eyes.

Mary Dazill watched her morosely, waiting till she had recovered her self-control. When Lucy turned back to her she found Mary's dark blue eyes fixed on her with a look that confused her with its understanding.

'Ah, yes,' said Mary, 'you were in love with him, too.'

Lucy bit her lip to suppress the renewed desire to weep that almost overcame her. 'You mean,' she said, '*you* were—?'

Mary Dazill closed her eyes for a moment; but when she opened them they were tearless as before. 'I suggest that you go back to the others,' she said coldly, 'and in future, curb your curiosity. You are too meddlesome by half.'

Lucy took a step forward. 'Do *you* know what happened to Leonard after he had left us all in the drawing-room? Did he say anything to *you?*'

'What do you mean?' said Mary Dazill. 'I never saw him again.'

'*I* did,' said Lucy.

'You did?'

'Yes. Oh, not in the way you think. I was left alone with him in the drawing-room, after you all went away. He didn't know I was there, at first. Then—he talked to me. That's why I came here. I'm sure—I'm sure he didn't shoot himself! How can he have, after what he said to me? He had no reason to—it wasn't as if he were in love with you—' She stopped, abruptly. Had she said too much? Mary Dazill was regarding her steadfastly.

'He told you that?' she said bitterly. 'How chivalrous!'

'Oh, no, no—not exactly,' cried out Lucy in distress. 'It wasn't like that at all. It just came out, that he was—'

'Playing a game of his own,' said Mary. 'Yes, I know.'

'You knew?'

'I said, "I know."'

'You mean, you've found out since?'

Mary Dazill gave a wry smile. 'I mean, I was being enlightened at the same time as yourself. Leonard's father explained everything to me quite clearly. As for Leonard himself, I am afraid I differ from you entirely. It seems to me he had every reason to shoot himself—if for no other reason, then from shame.'

'But he didn't—he didn't!' cried Lucy. 'I can prove it. Look here.' She ran behind the desk again, and dragged the heavy book across. 'Look at this.' She pointed to the spine. 'You see that hole? Now—' She opened the book at about the centre. Through the print ran a ragged furrow which buried itself in the thickness of the pages. Lucy turned them, frantically excited now. The furrow curved downward towards the binding. At last she reached its source. There in its paper bed lay a bullet. They both stared at it in amazement.

'You know where I found this book?' Lucy rounded on Mary Dazill almost accusingly. 'Behind that curtain there.'

'I see,' said Mary Dazill. 'And what do you imagine yourself to have proved?'

'I haven't *proved* anything,' retorted Lucy. 'And I don't suppose I ever can. I don't know, even, that I would if I could. But—I am certain Leonard didn't shoot himself, and this confirms it. I don't know who shot him or why. It may have been an accident—such things do happen, don't they, when people threaten more than they intend?'

'Go on,' said Mary Dazill, as Lucy turned to look at her.

'You see, a person standing in the doorway could fire a shot, merely to frighten—and the shot could end *there*, in among the books on that bookshelf underneath the window. And someone sitting here in the swivel-chair could turn and receive the second shot in his left temple—though it's hard to see how that could be accidental, too. Perhaps it was not accidental—perhaps the first shot was intended in earnest, and missed..."

'Perhaps,' said Mary Dazill, broodingly. 'You are a very clever girl, Lucy. I must think over what you say. Frankly, I think your imagination is running away with you. But—if I were you, I shouldn't make my surmises public, just in case your theory is right. In fact, I should keep them to myself.'

'Why?' said Lucy defiantly. 'If it's the truth, why shouldn't I reveal it?'

'Because, my dear Lucy, if we really have a murderer in our midst, your easiest method of shortening your own young life would be to let him know how clever you are.' She took Lucy by the elbow, and led her to the door. 'Now run away and don't waste any more thought upon it. You have been letting your mind dwell too long on sad things. Preoccupation with the past—it's a bad thing always, and for a young girl like you, absurd.'

Lucy resisted feebly. 'But what about the book?'

'Leave it to me. I shall put it back exactly where you found it, then we shall close up this room, and all it means to both of us, forever, Lucy.'

Lucy went off reluctantly down the corridor.

4

John paced nervously up and down the drawing-room carpet. He was flushed and angry. Lindy pretended to continue sewing placidly, as she had been doing when he entered; but she knew his dignity was badly hurt, and she feared a scene.

'It was a ridiculous idea,' he said. 'If I had known, I would never have come.' He swung round and faced her. 'Why didn't you tell me? I cannot imagine what you were thinking of.'

Lindy sewed on for a minute. There was a smile, not altogether kindly, on her lips. 'And she said nothing to you—not one word?'

John exclaimed angrily: 'The moment she saw me coming in through the door, she jumped up and rushed past me, out of the room. Don't ask me what was the matter with her. It wasn't anything I said or did, because she didn't give me time to speak.'

Lindy laid aside her work. The look she gave him was so long and so full of understanding that he had to avert his eyes. 'You mustn't be offended with Arran,' she said quietly. 'I assure you, she hasn't been at all herself lately. In fact, I have been very troubled about her. I thought perhaps a talk with *you* would do her good. But apparently the time for that has gone by.'

John blustered: 'I don't know what you mean.'

'I think you do, John,' said Lindy. 'I think you understand me very well.'

He came towards her, almost threateningly. 'I see! So this was a trap—and all under the guise of sisterly anxiety!'

'No,' said Lindy mildly. 'It wasn't a trap. You underestimate my—my pride, I assure you.' She turned and faced him squarely. 'Haven't *you* noticed anything odd about Arran lately? Haven't you seen any cause for anxiety? As for me, I have wondered if she were going out of her mind.'

John gave a harsh laugh. 'Her behaviour to-day, when I came in, would have confirmed your impression.'

'And you really feel no responsibility for it?'

'I? Certainly not! I'm not faintly interested in Arran. I can't help what the silly girl thinks she feels about me. But, Lindy, I should very much like to know what put this idea into your head—or who. Was it Arran?'

'Arran? John, don't be absurd. Arran has never breathed your name. Oh, no, it wasn't *she* who gave you away.'

'Then someone else has been talking.—Ah, yes, I know.' He nodded his head wisely, as he walked away. 'The snake in the grass! But if you really want an excuse for getting rid of me, Lindy, there are easier ways.' He came back to her. 'I think, after what you've just told me, I have the right to ask you to give me back my ring.'

Lindy turned pale. 'The *right?*' she murmured. 'Is that how you regard it?' She rose and went to the window. 'Will you please give me your reason?'

'You don't trust me,' muttered John. 'That's reason enough, for me.'

'No, no,' said Lindy, almost to herself. 'That is not your real reason. You are using that as a pretext. You wanted to marry me— and you have changed your mind. I wonder why. It isn't Arran, you say—and I believe you. No one could be so—blind, about someone they loved.' She turned to look at him, as if she were seeing him for the first time. 'And yet, you *have* changed. You've become—strange and secretive. You've lost all your old gaiety. I thought at first it must be because of—Leonard. I thought that was why you were avoiding us. But I see now, it began before then—Oh, no, it can't be!' she breathed. 'Not you, too! Is it witchcraft? What does she do to you all?'

She stared at him, fascinated. He made no denial. When Lucy Brown, full of her own strange experience, burst in upon them, she was unaware of having interrupted anything more than a desultory conversation.

Lucy was breathless, and flushed with excitement. Once out of Mary Dazill's sight, she had run the length of the whole corridor, and down the stairs. John and Lindy forgot their quarrel as she talked; one on each side of her, they listened to her in growing amazement.

'But, Lucy, it's fantastic!' said Lindy vigorously. 'Why, what you're saying is that someone *murdered* him!'

'I know, I know!' said Lucy. 'I know it sounds absurd. But—how did I conceive the idea in the first place? After all, I was the last to talk to him so far as we know; and if I got the impression then—I mean, if I felt afterwards, he had never had any intention of shooting himself, I must have got it from his own words, from the way he looked and spoke. And then, when something compelled me to go to his room and look—and I found what I did find—it doesn't look like fantasy, does it?'

'But,' said John, 'what makes you think this bullet—the one you found in the book—wasn't shot by Leonard himself? He might have missed the first time, and—'

'No,' interrupted Lucy vehemently. 'It's hard to explain, but—look, I will show you.' She went to one of the small tables that stood near the wall and brought it into the middle of the room. 'Now, John, suppose this is Leonard's desk. Bring a chair and sit at it, as he was doing. Now let this be the revolver.' She picked up, at random, an ivory fan lying on another small table. 'Point it—no, not with that hand: Leonard was left-handed, wasn't he?—point it at your left temple.'

John, somewhat reluctant, did so. But Lucy was indefatigable. She dragged one of the gilded satin-upholstered sofas across and placed it in front of John's table. 'This is Leonard's book-shelf under his window,' she announced. 'Now look where your revolver is pointing. If you missed—even supposing that were possible—where would the shot go? It would go in quite the opposite direction.'

'At right angles,' corrected John sourly.

'Yes—that's it. That's what I meant: at right angles, into the wall. And tell me—where would he have had to be standing if the bullet went into the book there?'

'Well, directly behind the desk, of course.'

'Exactly!' cried Lucy. 'And what is behind the desk? Do you remember?'

John shook his head. 'Nothing, so far as I know—except the chair.'

'Oh, but the shot couldn't have been fired by anyone sitting in the chair. It would have hit the edge of the desk, because the desk is fairly close to the bookshelf and the bookshelf is low down. But—farther back—what is there?'

'Nothing,' said John again. 'Nothing between the desk and the door.'

'The door!' cried Lucy. 'Don't you see? The shot could have
been fired by someone standing in the doorway. The first shot
missed. The second shot—as Leonard, turned in his swivel-chair—
struck him in the temple. The murderer then turned the body
round, so that it fell forward on to the desk, and laid the revolver
on the ground beside him. So you all thought Leonard had killed
himself. But I don't believe it. I don't believe it, and I never shall!'

'But, Lucy,' said Lindy anxiously, 'do you realise what you are
saying? You're saying that someone killed him—*some*one. You're
asking us to believe that a person exists, here in our midst, who
is capable of such a thing. The next step will be we shall have to
begin asking "*Who?*"'

Lucy came slowly back towards her. 'Well,' she said, 'can't you
imagine anyone in our midst who *would* be capable of it? I can.
I believe in the devil, and I believe he can enter into any one of
us, if we let him. That is where I am stronger than you, Lindy. We
have both led happy, protected lives, and we know very little about
the world; but *I* have been taught to believe in wickedness—in a
principle of evil at work in the world, against which we have to
fight without ceasing.' She spoke with the utmost earnestness.
Lindy was embarrassed, and looked down, waiting for her to finish.
John still sat where she had placed him, with his back to them, and
toyed with the ivory fan.

Lucy checked herself. She knew that missionary fervour was
not welcome here. The de Boulter family attended regularly the
service at her father's small, grey-towered church; but they drew
the line at any encroachment of religion on the other days of the
week. She changed her tone skilfully: 'But in spite of that, I must
say I think it would be best to let sleeping dogs lie. Supposing what
I say is true—who benefits? The truth would almost certainly be

so painful that anything would be better than knowing it—even the slur on poor Leonard's memory.' She cast a sidelong look at the back of John's head, to see how this affected him. 'In fact,' she went on, 'I suppose if we could have the truth revealed to us at this moment, we would do everything in our power to suppress it.'

John turned round at that. 'Oh, no,' he protested, 'I can't admit that. Look here, Lucy, if you know anything else, I think you're bound to tell us—tell me, at any rate, if Lindy doesn't feel able to stand it.'

'I can stand anything,' said Lindy, with a direct look at him. He averted his eyes.

'Yes. Well—well, what I mean is, I'm sure you're wrong, Lucy, but we're just as anxious as you are to protect Leonard's reputation. So tell me what you know, and I promise you I'll take care of the rest.'

Lucy smiled pityingly. 'I doubt if it would be as simple as that,' she said. 'But don't be afraid: I have told you everything, just as I came upon it myself. By the way—I suppose you know, both of you, that Mary Dazill was in love with Leonard?'

'What!' said Lindy; and John followed her with: 'How do you know?'

'She let it slip out while I was talking to her,' said Lucy importantly. 'So you see, you all had the affair quite wrong. Leonard was no more in love with her than—than with me. He was pretending to court her, to save you all from having her here as mistress of this house—as your father's wife. But she *was* in love with him—oh, deeply. She made that quite clear.' Lucy clasped her hands and sighed, unable to resist romance even when embodied in the enemy. 'And that opens up new vistas, doesn't it?' She got up. 'Good-bye.

I shall leave you two to talk it over. But as for me, I've fully made up my mind not to think about it any more.'

'Well,' said Lindy, as soon as she had gone. 'Would you have thought she had it in her? What a little busybody, to be sure!'

John, pacing up and down, nodded agreement.

'But what does she mean?' went on Lindy resentfully. 'Of course, I know it's all imagination—but what was she hinting at? You don't think she was trying to imply that—that Father—'

'Well,' said John, 'it sounded rather like that, didn't it?'

'Or,' continued Lindy, ignoring him, 'do you think she meant Mary Dazill? After all, she would be quite capable of murder, even, if she discovered that Leonard was playing a trick on her.'

John smiled maliciously. 'Yes, my dear,' he said, 'I agree with you there. I think she might be—especially as it was such a very caddish trick to play on anyone. You, being a woman, are bound to admit that.'

'John!' gasped Lindy, scandalised. But John was already at the door.

'Good-bye, Lindy,' he said. 'I'll come back to-morrow. I can see you're going to need me, to help you keep an eye on things. You will need to watch this Lucy Brown pretty closely, or she'll be having us all arrested on suspicion. How do we know she doesn't really suspect Arran—or you—or me?'

'Arran!' The name awoke Lindy to a sense of her duty. She remembered she had not seen her sister, or given her a thought, for an hour. What would be the effect of her misguided experiment? As soon as John had passed the window, she ran upstairs.

5

'And whom did your mother really suspect?' said Fitzbrown.

'Well,' said Mrs. Barratt, 'as you can imagine, it was always rather difficult to get her to say. She was a woman of strong religious principles, and charity was an article of faith with her, especially when the people concerned were dead. We used to ply her with questions, and she was extremely adept at evading them.'

'But all the same, she did say?'

'She allowed us to gather what she thought. She couldn't do much more in any case, since she never had any proof. But it was fairly clear to us that her suspicions alternated between Ralph de Boulter—the motive being jealousy, roused to madness when he discovered that Leonard had not only won Mary Dazill's love, but done so without wanting it—and Mary Dazill herself. Mary's motives would have been the fury of the woman scorned, when she discovered that Leonard's courtship was merely part of a plot against her; and perhaps the desire to protect her marriage with Ralph, which Leonard had sworn to prevent.'

'And which did she really believe?'

'Ah, that I can't say. Frankly, I think she would have become sensible in a few days, and have decided that she had invented the whole thing in the excitement of the moment. But something happened to confirm her in her view that Leonard's death was not what it seemed, and that there was danger lurking in wait for anyone who disputed appearances.

'One day, my mother had been as usual to call on Lindy, and was hurrying home...'

*

Twilight was closing in, as Lucy hurried across the drive, to the
wicket gate that led to the terrace. She had forgotten how soon
darkness fell, on these autumn evenings; and this evening the mists,
drifting in from the sea in long swathes, blotted out what little light
remained. She had not realised, when she left the house, what it
would be like outside. If she had known, she would have asked
Lindy to let one of the servants accompany her. Mr. de Boulter
had not been there; and John, having looked in and found the two
girls in close conversation, had left again.

Lucy's way took her round the back of the house, along the
terrace, and so by a path to a door in the boundary wall. From there,
it was only a few minutes' walk to the Vicarage. Oh, how glad she
would be to find herself through that gate, in the well-known lane!
She would not walk, this evening, she would run all the way to
the Vicarage garden gate, and in through the porch overhung with
Virginia creeper, through the friendly hall with its walls covered
with her father's collection of saddler's brass-work, into the cosy,
warm sitting-room where the fire leaped up the chimney and her
father sat reading and smoking... She groped for the wicket-gate.
Another great swathe of mist had come rolling in, and she could
no longer see the path by which she had come. The house loomed
darkly behind her; but it was no more than a shadow helping to
blot out the light. She could not distinguish the two stout columns
of the front porch by which she had left.

She fumbled for the latch, missing it at first in her eagerness.
She was not usually nervous or over-imaginative, like most girls.
Her work as the Vicar's daughter—and it was manifold, since her
mother had died many years ago—took her all over the village,
sometimes quite late at night; and she was used to going about
unattended. Who would harm Miss Lucy Brown, as she trotted

along with her basket, full of eggs and jellies for the invalids, on her arm, and her heart full of kind intention to all?

Now she was on the terrace. The house loomed up on her right hand, dark and silent: the heavy velvet curtains had all been drawn. On her left, though she could not see it, was the balustrade that flanked the terrace, and below that, the lawn with its trees, where they had sat in the spring and summer, that seemed so long ago.

The mist cleared for a moment: she saw the last wave of it floating wraith-like, past the angle of the house, and past the elm-tree avenue ahead of her. She must traverse that avenue before she reached the gate in the boundary-wall, the gate that seemed to her the very entrance to heaven, or at least to the earth of normal things, the life she knew. She prayed that the momentary break in the mist would last until she could reach there.

She came to the west wing, below the round tower in which Leonard's room had been, and stood for a minute, looking ahead into the darkness of the avenue. Then she braced herself to go forward. She could see rolling up on her left hand another great bank of mist, that blotted out all landmarks in its passage. Again she hesitated, wondering if she should turn back. Then, for the last time, she made up her mind, and plunged with bowed head and hurrying feet into the obscurity of the avenue.

She had not reached the second of the great elm trees when a slight sound seemed to disturb the air quite close to her ear; and a sharp click followed, as if something had struck the tree ahead of her. She continued to run forward, almost colliding with the tree; and at that distance, she saw something that jutted out from it— something stiffer and straighter than a branch, yet still quivering, although there was surely not enough wind to stir it. She put out her hand to touch the strange object; and as she did so, a thrill of fear ran through her. Yet she would not relinquish it. She tugged frantically, until it came away in her hand...

When, some ten minutes later, Lucy rushed sobbing into the vicarage sitting-room, carrying in her hand a long feathered arrow, her father patted her hair and soothed her.

'But, my darling,' he said, 'why didn't you get someone to come with you? Why, if I had known you'd come by yourself through the mist,—but I felt sure that Lindy would keep you there. As for the arrow—look, its point is quite rusted. It must be an old one, left there after one of your archery matches.'

'But, Father,' sobbed Lucy, 'I heard it—I heard it fly past my ear! And I heard it strike the tree. It was still vibrating when I touched it!'

'There, there,' he said. 'Go to bed and don't think about it any more. The mist can play strange tricks with one's sight and hearing. You heard a twig crack under your foot, perhaps, and then you saw the arrow sticking in the tree—and your mind linked the two things together. Ah, yes, the mind is a wonderful piece of mecha-nism—sometimes *too* quick for our interpretative powers...' He went off into a reverie on one of his favourite subjects.

Lucy was much too wise to argue, or trouble him with all the thousand wild surmises that thronged through her own mind. It was just as well that he chose to take it so... She dried her eyes, kissed him good night, and went away, still carrying the arrow.

6

For a while, Lucy Brown told no one of her experience. Indeed, in the cold light of morning she almost doubted if it had occurred. True, she still had the arrow which she had wrenched from the elm tree; but was her father's explanation perhaps the right one? She took the arrow to the window, and standing in a square of sunshine, examined it carefully; but it revealed nothing. It was merely one of the set of arrows they had used for their archery. The haft, she noticed, was slightly warped; she wondered if she owed her life to that. The metal arrow-head was rusted, but not deeply: the arrow could not have been one of those left lying about out of doors, or the head would have been encrusted. This was only a film of rust, such as gathers on anything made of steel, even indoors...

Even indoors! And then it struck her where she had last seen the archery equipment. The target was still in its old place, under the trees. But the bows and arrows—they had been standing in a corner, in Leonard's room!

Her mind flew to the last time—the first and last—she had stood there. The windows overlooked the terrace—commanded the entrance to the avenue. It was an ideal place from which to take aim. Was it possible? Yes, indeed it was—if Lucy, stumbling on a murderer's secret, had herself been surprised...

Trembling, she stared at the arrow with renewed horror. It had been meant for her heart. She remembered how it had sounded as it sped past her ear and stuck vibrating in the bark of the great elm tree. She held it here in her hand, a captive; and yet it could tell her nothing of that other murderous hand which had sent it forth on its death-errand. A fact so tangible, so recent, ought to leave traces, if only one could read them. But the traces, if they existed, were invisible.

Gradually, as she stood there before her bedroom window with its pretty flowered curtains, and gazed across the peaceful vicarage garden, her mind became calm and clear again. She would say nothing, this time, even to Lindy. But she was not going to be frightened away. From here, she could see in the distance the tops of the elm trees that bordered the avenue which she had trodden last night in such inexplicable fear. Yes, she would go back—but she would no longer be trusting and confiding; and moreover, the hidden enemy should never again catch her alone, or in the dark, or with her back turned.

It was a few days later. Again they were in the drawing-room; but it was afternoon, and Lucy had not taken off her bonnet. She had called ostensibly on some trivial parish business, actually because she judged that if she stayed away any longer it would become noticeable. Also, she was curious: she could not believe that what had happened the other night, in the mist, would not somehow have made itself felt in this household. But when she arrived, she found a state of affairs more peaceful and normal than she had seen since Leonard's death; Lindy was presiding at the table, John was helping her, Mary Dazill sat by the window; and best of all, Arran, so long absent from family gatherings, was lying on the sofa. She looked pale and ill, and changed in some indefinable way: not older—she was too young to look anything but the age she was—but lost, frightened, helpless—or was it bewildered? Formerly she had been, in her quiet way, a rather self-willed young creature; one would have thought that it would have taken more than a disappointment in love, or even a family tragedy, to crush her spirit. It was pathetic, therefore, to see how dependent she had become on Lindy; her eyes followed Lindy's every movement, and she seemed scarcely to see anyone else in the room. When John brought her a cup of tea she seemed at first unaware of his nearness, because her gaze was still fixed on Lindy; then, when he gently drew her attention to himself, she started back in alarm. Lindy had to get up and go to her, pretending to rearrange the pillow at her back, and the rug over her knees, in order to restore her.

Lucy kept manfully to her resolve, to say nothing about the mysterious arrow. But it cost her a great effort, and if she could have been left alone with Lindy for a few minutes, she would probably have flung her caution to the winds, and poured out the whole story. As it was, she listened to the placid conversation going on about the weather, the new chrysanthemums in the greenhouse, the number of bunches of grapes the various vines had borne this season as compared with last; and once again, she wondered if she had invented the whole story. Even Mary Dazill joined in the conversation occasionally. She was being treated with great deference. John, as he waited on her, devoured her with his eyes; Lindy seemed unaware of anything but her duties as a hostess; both asked her her opinion on this and that whenever possible. She answered briefly; but for the most part she seemed to prefer to gaze out of the window, lost in her own thoughts. Beyond an acknowledgment of Lucy's 'good afternoon' when she entered, Mary Dazill took no further notice of Lucy.

All seemed to be going well, when suddenly the door was flung open, and Ralph de Boulter confronted them all. Lucy had not seen him since the day of the funeral; and she was shocked at his appearance. His hair had gone much greyer; his complexion was as fresh as ever, and he held himself just as squarely; but all trace of his former *bonhomie* had vanished, and his vigour seemed to have turned to violence. When he spoke, his voice was harsh and full of fury:

'Ah,' he said, 'I am glad to find you all here. I have something to say to you.'

They all stared at him in fascinated horror, aware that he was about to make a most disagreeable scene—all, that is, except Mary

Dazill, who, after one glance at him, had turned away and resumed her reverie, as if what was happening had not the slightest interest for her. Ralph glared round the circle: his eyes lit on Lucy, and stopped there.

'And you, Miss Brown,' he said. 'I am particularly glad to see *you* in my house—but I am afraid I shall not be able to extend that welcome much longer, unless you stop meddling and tattling and inventing absurd stories.'

Lucy rose. The sudden attack took her completely unawares, and her head reeled under the blow. But she rallied all her forces, and, though scarlet with shame and anger, managed to say quietly:

'I don't understand you, Mr. de Boulter. But I should be very sorry to stay in anybody's house a moment longer than I am welcome.'

'Father!' called out Lindy. 'Lucy, please don't go! Father, you mustn't let her!'

Ralph de Boulter stared uncertainly at the small advancing figure of Lucy. His tall form blocked the doorway; but she appeared quite prepared to push him out of the way, when they were both arrested by the cool, incisive voice of Mary Dazill:

'Ralph, don't be so stupid.'

Ralph gasped; and even Lucy, angry as she was, turned in surprise. Mary crossed the room towards them.

'Are you out of your senses?' she said scornfully to Ralph. 'Don't you realise that Miss Brown has no idea what you are talking about? You can't speak to her like that.' She turned to Lucy. 'You must excuse Mr. de Boulter, Lucy,' she said. 'He is deeply disturbed. He doesn't mean what he has just said to you.'

'Oh yes, he does,' replied Lucy, with spirit. 'What you mean is, I am now to hear an explanation of it—in other words, I am to stand here and hear it repeated with additions. Thank you, no.'

She turned again to the door. It was Lindy's hand on her arm that stopped her.

'Please, Lucy!' Lindy spoke in a rapid murmur, so that the others could not hear. 'Don't leave me—yet. I have enough to bear—I can't—' Tears glistened in her eyes. Lindy did not easily cry or ask for favours. Lucy could not resist the appeal. She threw dignity to the winds; and besides, curiosity pricked her. She turned and faced Ralph de Boulter.

'You have something further to say to me?'

Ralph, baffled and daunted by all this unexpected support for Lucy, said irritably:

'Oh, for God's sake, Mary, *you* explain it to her. After all, it was you who told me.'

Lucy turned to Mary. 'Oh, I see! You have been carrying tales! I might have known—'

Mary Dazill studied her coldly. 'My dear Lucy, I told Mr. de Boulter of your discovery, that is all. I showed him the evidence you showed me. Don't you think it right that he should know? Leonard was his son, you know.'

Ralph interrupted. 'Yes, yes. I apologise to you, Miss Brown, for speaking as I did just now. But this idea—it upset me. It's preposterous. You must put it out of your head immediately. No good can come of such prying—into the affairs of the dead. Let my son sleep in peace. If he had secrets, I prefer not to know them.'

Lucy watched him curiously, listened to the note of fear in his voice, and thought: 'Is this the man who has travelled far and wide, and braved so many dangers? What can have happened to him? Is it—can it be a guilty conscience? But if it were, would he go out of his way to display it to us all?'

'I'm sorry,' she said gently. 'If you feel like that, I can't, of course, say anything against it—except that I should have thought, if it were true—*if* it were true—one would want to know—one might think the person who had died had the right to have his name vindicated. He might almost ask such a thing of the people who had loved him.'

Ralph made a violent gesture of denial.

'But that is only my idea,' continued Lucy calmly, 'and I have no right to press it, against your wishes. So please don't let it trouble you any further. It's—dead and buried, so far as I am concerned.'

She wondered if she had chosen the right words. Mary Dazill was looking at her disdainfully.

'You see, Ralph?' she said. 'Miss Brown is wholly accommodating. So set your mind at rest. We will all forget the matter as quickly as possible. After all, what does it concern Leonard? He is dead, and can easily bear the blame, if it saves us any little embarrassment.' She walked toward the door. 'Come, Ralph. You have said enough.'

She was gone, leaving them all staring after her. The moment she was out of hearing, Ralph seemed to recover his self-confidence.

'Then it's understood?' he said, looking round the circle. 'None of you will mention this any further—not even to one another.' He seemed to see John for the first time, and added with ghastly facetiousness: 'By the way, John, when is the wedding to be? Young men were more impatient in my young days. If you don't make up your mind, I shall be before you yet.'

His over-hearty laugh was not echoed. When he had gone, there was an audible sigh of relief. But a moment later, a stifled cry from the sofa recalled them: Arran lay back on her pillow, pale and still. She had fainted.

7

'The strange slow mental sickness,' continued Mrs. Barratt, 'which had been devouring Arran since Leonard died, now took a turn for the worse. After her fainting attack, they carried her to bed; but when she revived, it seemed as if she awoke to a world of nightmare. She tossed and moaned, and seemed to dread opening her eyes. A doctor was called; but he was frankly puzzled. He could find nothing wrong with her physically; and after shaking his head a good deal, and asking some very significant questions, he had a private talk with her father and told him that he feared for the balance of her mind. It was assumed by both of them that the shock of Leonard's death was the cause of the trouble... Lindy and my mother took it in turns to watch her for the first few days. My mother said she talked a good deal in her sleep, or delirium; but it was impossible to make out what she was saying. Now and again, a name would stand out from among a murmured rush of unintelligible words: John, or Lindy, or Lucy, and once or twice, even 'Leonard!' in a voice of terror and agony. But she never mentioned her father, or Mary Dazill. John, remorseful no doubt at his share in her suffering, called every day with anxious inquiry, and presents of fruit and flowers. But they did not repeat the experiment of allowing him to see her.

'At last, slowly she seemed to rally; at any rate, she became quieter. Her restless days and nights gave place to long hours of sleep, or of quietness when she would be staring ahead of her blankly, without a word, without a sign that she was aware of any past or any future, without a clue to what she was thinking, if she was thinking at all. In these periods, they made no attempt to disturb her, or recall her to her surroundings. But it was a relief to them to find her calm again; and after a week of constant nursing, they were gradually able to relax their attention. She began to show signs of noticing their presence; and when at last she rewarded their efforts with an occasional smile, they were overjoyed. Once, at the outset, Mary Dazill came and offered to sit up with her for part of the night; but Lindy refused this offer, with as much politeness as she could muster. Leave her dear sister alone with a stranger? Never! And my mother, thinking of that strange experience of hers in the avenue of elms, supported Lindy in this decision. Mary Dazill shrugged her shoulders and went away.

'But now, when Arran was sleeping at night again without the help of a sleeping-draught, and the doctor said that with care she would probably soon be well enough to try the only possible cure—a change of air—something happened to shatter their hopes once more…'

It was a wild, gusty evening in November. Lucy was preparing to go home. During Arran's illness, she had subordinated all her fears to her devotion to the sick; but still, she had contrived never to go unescorted along the elm-tree avenue after dark. Either she had stayed the night, and watched by Arran's bed, to spare Lindy; or she had left while it was still daylight. Sometimes she even accepted John's escort, at Lindy's suggestion; but she never mentioned to either of them that she had any grounds for alarm. As she passed the elm tree in which the arrow had lodged, a thrill of recollected fear would run through her; but she repressed the temptation to talk about it. One day, when she passed by here in the daylight alone, she could not help stopping to look and see if she could find the scar where the point of the arrow had penetrated. But the bark was old and gnarled, and the hole had evidently healed over, or become coated with the green protective film of moss. The only tangible proof of her adventure was the rusty arrow, which she still kept in a bedroom cupboard at home.

'It's late,' said Lindy as they came down the stairs together. 'And how dark it's getting! The evenings are drawing in. Won't you stay and have dinner with us?'

'No, no, thank you,' said Lucy apprehensively. Against the tall window at the junction of the double stairway the wind was hurling itself in thunderous gusts, and she could see how quickly twilight had fallen. Yet she did not want to betray her nervousness to Lindy. 'Of course, if you would like me to sit with Arran to-night—'

'Oh, no, dear,' said Linda cheerfully. 'It won't be necessary for us to do that any longer. I hope. In fact, Doctor Merriman said I needn't sleep in her room to-night. He said it would be better to leave her alone—and better for me to get some real rest, too.'

'Very well,' Lucy said resignedly. There was nothing for it— she must pull the hood of her cloak up over her head and run the whole way, looking neither to right nor left—and certainly not behind. 'Like one that on a lonesome road'—inevitably the lines ran through her brain—'doth walk in fear and dread, and having once looked back, walks on and turns no more his head—because he fears'—what? What?

How relieved she felt when she heard the familiar ring at the front door bell, and a moment later a maid crossed the hall to open the door to John.

'Ah, here's John,' cried Lindy. 'He will take you. John dear, will you please take Lucy home before you settle down? It's rather late for her to go along the avenue.'

'Of course I will,' said John, handing Lindy a large bunch of chrysanthemums, and taking back his hat and stick from the maid.

'Oh, how lovely!' Lindy inhaled the bitter scent of the magnificent incurved white blooms. 'John, you *must* give them to her yourself. I suppose they *are* for Arran and not for me?' Since she had known for certain that John's straying affections had not alighted on Arran, she longed above all things to re-establish the old friendly relationship between them. 'Do come, just for a minute. She will be so pleased.' She turned to lead him back up the staircase, and after a moment's hesitation he followed. Lucy remained behind, impatient to be gone.

They were away for a considerable time. Then John reappeared at the head of the stairs. 'Lucy,' he said in an agitated voice, 'will you come up here, please?'

She joined him. 'Arran is not in her room,' he said. 'We can't find her anywhere. We've looked in Lindy's room and everywhere in the tower. She didn't come down the stairs, did she?'

'No,' said Lucy, wondering.

'Well!' he led her back towards Arran's and Lindy's tower, 'where else can she have got to?'

'Have you asked her father?'

'I did tap on his study door, but there was no reply.'

'And Miss Dazill?' Lucy gave him a straight look.

'Oh, I—I can't very well disturb *her*...' They were passing Mary's door at that moment, and John cast a fearful sidelong look at it.

'Why not?' Lucy was beginning, when the door opened, and Mary Dazill came out.

'Is anything the matter?' she said. 'I heard voices.' Her tone was chiding, as if to say: 'Must you be so excitable and noisy?'

'Yes, indeed there is, Miss Dazill,' replied Lucy energetically. 'Arran is not in her room, and I am just going along to help Lindy to look for her.'

She bustled on, leaving John to confront Mary's ironic smile. He gazed at her helplessly, made as if to say something, changed his mind, and let her pass. She went slowly down the corridor and away; for since her offer of help had been refused, she had made no attempt to renew it. But before she reached the head of the staircase, she called to Lucy:

'Miss Brown.'

Her voice was low, but Lucy turned as if commanded to halt.

'Why not try the other wing? She may have had the same idea as yourself, you know—or perhaps something you have said has suggested it.' She paused, while Lucy waited on tenterhooks. 'She passed me just now, apparently going in that direction.'

'And you didn't stop her?' cried Lucy, appalled.

'Why should I?' said Mary Dazill, nonchalantly. 'She might have resented it, as you would have done; and with even more justice, as she is in her father's house.'

'But,' said Lucy, 'she's—she's ill. She's in no state to be left to wander about alone.'

By this time, John had come up. Mary Dazill looked at him before answering:

'She certainly has something on her mind,' she said with a smile. 'But it's something she can't speak about, that's all. She is not mad, as you are all trying to maintain—though if you persist in treating her as mad, she may become so.'

She turned away, and went slowly down the stairs. John stood gazing after her, as if afraid to follow, yet unable to go away. Lucy shook his arm.

'Come on!' she said. 'We must look for her. She mustn't be left alone in Leonard's room.'

'No,' said John, 'no, of course not.' But as he followed Lucy, he still looked backward, though Mary had disappeared from his sight.

They hurried together along the corridor, Lucy pattering quickly, John striding beside her. The door of Leonard's room stood open; they paused for a moment on the threshold, and took in the scene: Arran, in her nightdress and wrap, her long fair hair lying in ringlets on each shoulder, was bending down behind Leonard's desk, rummaging in the bookcase. A pile of books lay beside her.

She turned as Lucy approached her. 'It's gone!' she gasped, as if continuing a conversation. Then she stood up, and seeing them both, seemed suddenly to realise where she was and what she was doing: at any rate, a look of terror crossed her face, her smooth young brow furrowed in a frown, her hand went to her mouth; and before Lucy had time to get to her, she had given a queer little cry and sunk in a heap on the floor.

8

A deep chuckle came from the corner: 'As if she had seen a ghost,' said Superintendent Mallett. '*I* know.'

They looked at him in surprise. 'Why, that's very strange,' said Mrs. Barratt. 'Those were the very words my mother used to me. How did you know?'

'Oh, well,' said Mallett, 'I just thought, perhaps she had, you know.'

'Had *what?*' said Dr. Fitzbrown.

'Seen a ghost,' said Mallett. He gave another chuckle and took to his pipe and his silence again. They all gazed at him, hoping for some explanation, but it was clear that none would be forthcoming. Mrs. Barratt continued:

'After that, as you can imagine, there was a state of consternation in the house. At first, nobody quite foresaw the consequences. All was forgotten in the bustle of carrying poor Arran back to her bed, sending for the doctor, arranging for night nursing, and so on. My mother found herself permanently installed again; and gradually, as their lives—hers and Lindy's—began to revolve once more round Arran's sickroom, two things began to emerge with startling clarity—the intense hatred with which Lindy regarded Mary Dazill; and the change for the worse in Ralph de Boulter.'

Arran had gone to sleep again. Her coming-round after the fainting attack had been uneventful: she had simply opened her eyes, gazed at them, and sighed. With consciousness, a slight look of fear returned; but she said nothing. Two tears rolled down her pale cheeks. Lucy felt her own eyes filling in sympathy; but Lindy's look was stern and hard.

After the doctor's visit, it was decided that Lindy and Lucy should take it in turns to spend the night with her; but for a while they sat watching together, and when they were sure that the sleeping-draught had taken effect, they began a whispered conversation:

'She must have been listening, much more than we realised,' said Lucy. 'It must have preyed on her mind, until in the end she had to go and see for herself.'

'And Mary Dazill helped her,' said Lindy.

'Oh, Lindy, we can't be sure of that,' deprecated Lucy. 'She merely saw her going, and didn't stop her.'

'It's almost as bad,' Lindy retorted. 'It makes her responsible for—this.' She brooded for a while, and the flickering night-light threw dark shadows across her face. 'I wonder—I believe she knows more about all this than any of us. Why was it she who found you there, and interrupted you, that first time? Perhaps—' Her dark eyes flashed as the possibilities began to occur to her.

'Perhaps what?' said Lucy cautiously. She wanted to see if Lindy's conjectures would in any way support her own, before she gave away her secret.

'Perhaps it was she—she who killed my brother!' Lindy's excitement was rising. 'I never doubted that it was in some way due to her—everything has gone wrong since she came here—but I mean, perhaps she actually took a revolver and shot him.'

'Surely she wouldn't be capable!'

'Oh yes, she would. She is capable of anything. Look how she has come here and made herself mistress of the place—captivated my father—coolly planned everything for her own advantage. As for John, he's her slave. Oh, don't trouble to deny it—I know all about John. She shot Leonard, because he planned to wreck her marriage, and therefore her future. She thinks only of herself. She is the cold, calculating type who lets nothing stand in her way.'

'Not even love?' said Lucy. 'After all, she loved Leonard.'

'That made no difference, if he didn't love her. In fact, it would make her even more furious against him. Lucy, we must get rid of her. We *must*. If we don't, we are all lost. I feel it. There's something about her—oh, how I hate her! I hate her!'

'Hush, Lindy,' said Lucy, scandalised. She herself disliked Mary Dazill, and feared her; but she could not allow the use of such expressions, not without protesting, even if Mary were the devil himself. 'You mustn't speak like that. You have no proof of what you say.'

'Proof?' said Lindy. 'What more do you want? It was you who discovered that Leonard had been shot, by someone standing in the doorway—and you who found the book with the bullet in it. She didn't know about that herself, until she caught you there. And now what happens? The book is missing! Who but herself would want to go back and destroy it? She was afraid lest one of us should investigate further—so she destroyed the only piece of evidence.'

A chill struck through Lucy: she seemed to hear Mary Dazill's cold voice saying:...'and in future curb your curiosity. You are too meddlesome by half.'

'The wonder is,' went on Lindy, 'she didn't destroy the only witness—you. I suppose she would have, if she could have done it without being caught.'

Lucy gasped. 'Oh, Lindy,' she said tremblingly, 'I wish you hadn't said that.'

'Why?' Lindy was all attention.

'Because—well, I didn't mean ever to tell a soul. I can't bear to think that anyone could be so wicked—and yet—'

'Plenty of people are,' said Lindy.

Lucy shook her head: on this question, they seemed to have changed sides. But she could no longer resist the temptation to confide. In whispers, across Arran's still form, she told Lindy the strange adventure in the elm avenue, when the arrow—now, she was sure, deliberately aimed—missed her by a few inches.

'I still can't believe it, Lindy,' she ended. 'And yet, as you say, if she were guilty, she might think I knew more than I did. And it's true she could have aimed the arrow from Leonard's room. We know she could handle the bow as well as any of us, in spite of her pretence of helplessness—and one of the bows was kept there.'

'Yes. Yes,' Lindy whispered back. 'Oh, why didn't you tell me sooner? Your life has been in danger, all this while—and now Arran's. It must have been she who talked to my father and got him to make that scene when he accused you of interfering.'

'I wondered at the time, in spite of her denial,' admitted Lucy. 'That was why I said so pointedly that, so far as I was concerned, the affair was closed, if *he* didn't wish the truth to be investigated.'

'But you didn't mean it?'

'No. But I didn't want to be killed.'

Lindy clasped her hands. 'What are we to do? What are we to do?' she said aloud.

Arran stirred and moaned in her sleep.

9

Next morning, Lindy awoke from a short sleep to hear a tapping on the door. A maid entered: her manner conveyed to Lindy that there was fresh trouble brewing.

'Please, Miss Lindy, the master says will you come downstairs at once? He wishes to speak to you. He will be leaving in half an hour.'

'Leaving? My father?' Lindy could not believe her ears. She was too dazed with yesterday's happenings, and lack of sleep, to be able to refrain from asking: 'Where is he going?'

The maid looked wooden. 'I'm sure I don't know, Miss. He came down and ordered breakfast in a great hurry, and the dog-cart to be outside by half-past eight. I think he's catching the train.'

Lindy controlled herself. 'Very well, I shall come at once.'

She dressed quickly. She had seen so little of her father lately, that she had forgotten how to speak to him. What a difference there was between the handsome, soldierly-looking man who had at once captured her romantic admiration, and this distracted, harsh, dangerous man who held the future of all of them in his hands! Her awe and admiration had changed to fear.

Her heart beat fast as she entered the room. He was standing on the hearth-rug, with his overcoat and gloves on, impatiently waiting to go.

'Ah, Lindy,' he said. 'Come here. I am going up to town for a couple of days, and I have one or two things to say to you. I want you to think about them in my absence.'

'Yes, Father,' said Lindy, her apprehension growing.

'I am going,' he said in his loud, defiant tone, 'in the first place to arrange about the marriage-settlement, and other money matters connected with it. These things have now reached completion: they require my signature only. But while I am there, I may as well discuss your affairs, too.'

'My affairs?' faltered Lindy.

'Yes, yes,' he said impatiently, 'your marriage. My—plans for the future won't affect my provision for you. I'm prepared to make the original settlement, a very generous one, I consider. I went over to see John's parents yesterday, and—'

'But, Father, interrupted Lindy, 'you don't understand. You don't know what has been happening since—' she, had meant to say, 'since you've become a recluse,' but did not dare. The truth must be spoken, however, cost what it may: 'I—I don't know whether John and I still wish to marry each other.'

The effect was as she had expected: 'What?' said Ralph. 'What nonsense is this? He was your own choice, wasn't he? You told me you could think of no greater happiness in life than to marry him, when you asked me to give him my consent. If it's a lovers' quarrel, you'll soon make it up. Meanwhile, this business of mine can't wait. You must realise, you're a woman now, not a child. Marriage is a serious matter.'

'Yes,' murmured Lindy.

Ralph scraped his throat. 'My own marriage,' he said,'will take place in six weeks' time. Now, Lindy—I have pretty good reason for thinking that when John next calls, he will ask you to name the day.'

'You've spoken to John?' said Lindy, appalled.

'No, no,' said Ralph testily. 'Not to him—to his father. But what I want to say to you, Lindy, is—you may fix the date as soon as you please—say a couple of months hence. I don't approve of long engagements between young people.'

Lindy's temper began to rise. 'You mean, Father,' she said, drawing herself up, 'you want to get rid of me as soon as you are married.'

'Well,' answered Ralph, not so angrily as she had expected, 'you've made no great attempt to make yourself pleasant to Mary, have you? You can hardly expect her to want you here when she's the mistress. Not that she has said so: the idea is mine. I won't have my life made intolerable at home by women's squabbles. So I'm afraid you'll have to go, Lindy. After all, it's no great hardship: you are merely leaving this house for a home of your own, as you would wish to do in any case. I'm not going to turn you out into the world—though sometimes I think it would be a good thing for you.'

'But, Father,' said Lindy, 'what about Arran? *She* has nowhere to go—and besides, she's ill, desperately ill. You can't turn *her* out—and I shall have to stay, to look after her. I would never leave,' she added with growing vehemence, 'while Arran needed me.'

Ralph seemed about to answer angrily; but he checked himself. 'Now look here, Lindy,' he said, 'you are exaggerating this illness of Arran's, because it gives you something to do. But it can't go on indefinitely like this. Arran was a strong, healthy girl until after her brother's death—and she'll be a strong, healthy girl again, when her *mind* recovers from the shock.' His slight emphasis on the word 'mind' did not escape Lindy. He turned, as the sound of horses' hooves outside attracted his attention to the window; the dog-cart passed, and they could hear its harness jingling as it pulled up in front of the porch.

'As a matter of fact,' he went on, picking up his hat from a table, and going to the door, 'that is one of the things I want to see about when I'm in town. I intend to consult a mental specialist about her—and if I can find the right man, I shall arrange for an examination. You'd better prepare her—I may bring him back with me. Don't mention the word "mental," of course; just tell her a doctor, or a nerve-specialist, or anything else you please.'

Lindy stood in his path. 'And what then?' she said.

'Well, if he finds any—er—mental weakness, we shall have to send her away for a while, to a suitable place, where they know how to deal with these things.'

'You mean an asylum?' said Lindy.

'No, no, of course not! There are plenty of places—homes, where she can have supervision and proper nursing. Now don't argue with me, Lindy: that is what I have decided.'

'Yes, Father,' said Lindy, standing aside.

He gave her a perfunctory kiss on the forehead, and left hastily, relieved that this very awkward interview was over. But if he could have seen Lindy, white-faced, tense, still standing where he had left her, staring after him, he might have had less cause to feel satisfied.

I O

'How the next few days passed,' said Mrs. Barratt, 'the days of Ralph's absence, my mother did not know. She was called home because of the sudden illness of her father; and so she could no longer help Lindy to nurse Arran. But one can imagine that they passed uneasily, now that there was no one to stand between Lindy and Mary Dazill...'

Lindy stood on the roof of her turret, watching Mary Dazill, as she walked below, along the terrace in the winter's sunshine. She and Mary had exchanged hardly a word since her father left; they sat together at meals, forced to be polite for as long as the servants were in the room; and when they were left alone, an icy silence fell. This silence—Mary Dazill was a past master in the art of it. By means of it, she could reduce Lindy almost to hysteria; yet she herself remained self-possessed and calm.

'How I hate her!' thought Lindy, unable to move away from the parapet. The sight of the small neat figure, so very much alone, aroused in her a feeling of baffled fury. To think that already she was mistress of all this—she, the intruder! If only something would happen—anything, anything, to remove her! Accidents did happen: why couldn't one happen now? A loose coping-stone, perhaps, dislodged by a gust of wind... If it had been in Lindy's power to send such a stone toppling over, could she have resisted? She was not sure.

And now, what was going to happen, when her father came back? There would be a few weeks' preparation, in which, no doubt, she, Lindy, would be expected to play her part. She would have to sit in church and hear the reading of the banns: 'If any of you know cause, or just impediment—' She would have to bear with the curiosity of neighbours, the endless gossip, the watchful eyes... When would he send Arran away? Before the wedding, naturally: he would not want her in the house, to remind him of his duty. Perhaps he would want to get rid of Lindy too. Or would her usefulness outweigh her unpleasant associations for him? Yes, undoubtedly she would be expected to stay, if only for convention's sake...

Round and round went Lindy's thoughts, in agonised anxiety. She thought: 'If this goes on, I shall go mad.' And then it struck her: 'Is that what he wants—to drive us both mad, and so get rid of us?' No, she thought, probably he would prefer the easier plan, of hurrying on her marriage to John. He had been to see John's parents; he had discussed the marriage-settlement. At this thought, once again her cheeks burned. The parents would have spoken to John—and he would have had to lie, or else betray his change of mind. He had not been near her since her father had gone away. But one thing was certain: she would never marry him, knowing of him what she did. No, she would follow Arran into this madhouse they were planning for her, or throw herself on the mercy of some convent, or Sisters of Charity. Better to work among lepers than to submit to such degradation. Her father could storm and bluster: she might have a surprise in store for him yet.

Well, it would not be long now: she would not have to endure this torment much longer. A curt note from her father had arrived that morning, saying that he would be back this evening, and telling her to have the dog-cart sent to meet the train... Yes, she had loved her father: when she had seen him, for the first time since childhood, she had thought him all that a man should be—handsome, strong, good-tempered, kind. But now in his infatuation—his treachery as she saw it—he seemed to her contemptible; and she hated him for having destroyed her dream.

*

A light step on the stone staircase that led up to the turret roof startled her; she was still more startled to see Arran's head appear. Arran was pale, but composed. It was so long since she had left her own room that Lindy ran towards her in alarm, afraid lest a breath of wind should blow her away. But Arran needed no help. Slowly she made her way round between the sloping tiled roof and the battlemented parapet, to where Lindy had been standing. The wind stirred her fair brown curls, and brought colour to her cheeks; she leaned against the stone-work, and gazed out over the garden, across the tops of the trees, to the silver line of the sea.

'So we are to leave here,' she said at last.

Lindy caught her breath, wondering how Arran knew. 'Yes,' she said hastily, 'but not yet. There will be plenty of time for arrangements to be made—and we shall be together—it won't be so bad—'

Arran stared out into the distance. 'You needn't try to deceive me,' she said. 'I know quite well what he plans. He believes—or wants to believe—I'm mad, doesn't he? He intends to send me away, where *you* won't be able to follow me.'

'Who told you that?' cried Lindy in a fury. She leaned over to look down on to the terrace-walk; but it was empty. Mary Dazill was no longer there to be the unwitting object of her hatred.

'I know,' said Arran calmly. 'It was in his voice when he came to see me, before he went away; and it has been in your face ever since. But I shan't go—that is, unless *you* want to get rid of me too.'

'Arran, darling!' Lindy was appalled. 'You know that nothing—nothing in the world—would make me leave you! 'Don't say such terrible things!'

Arran turned to gaze at her. She looked now, Lindy thought, as beautiful as an angel, with her blue eyes fringed with long lashes, and her pallor, and her gravity. In these last six months, she had changed beyond measure.

'Not even John?' she said.

'What?' Lindy did not understand for a moment. 'Oh—make me leave you. No, not even John.' She laughed a little. 'Though I hardly think you need be afraid of *him*. He has shown no sign of wanting to tear me from you.'

Arran laid a hand on Lindy's arm, and gripped it with such strength that Lindy was surprised. 'Listen,' she said, 'I want you to promise me one thing.'

'Why, of course, dear—anything you please,' said Lindy soothingly. The look in Arran's eyes alarmed her, and her heart beat fast with a sudden misgiving.

'Promise me,' said Arran, 'you will never marry John.'

Lindy gazed at her, astonished. 'Never marry John?' she faltered. 'But, Arran, dear, you—you can hardly ask me that. I mean—probably, I think almost certainly, I never shall, knowing what I do of him. But—ought *you* to be the one to ask it?'

Arran was unmoved. She seemed not to understand Lindy's question. 'Promise you won't,' she repeated fiercely, 'whatever they say, all of them—Father, his family, everybody. If you don't, I shall throw myself over the parapet.'

Lindy's thoughts moved quickly. There was no doubt in her mind that Arran meant what she said. But why—why? Lindy had reconciled herself to the loss of John, though somewhere, deep in her, was still the hope that he might return to his old self, once Mary Dazill was safely married. Yet she did not wish to make this promise. She hated to throw away her freedom of choice—and how could Arran of all people bring herself to ask it? It seemed to Lindy, hard though she tried to make allowances, a strangely unfair demand; and it was strangely unlike Arran to make it. Yes, that was it! It was utterly out of character. It was not Arran's nature to want to snatch somebody else's happiness in that crude way; nor was she one of those who are determined to prevent others from getting what they cannot get for themselves. Then had she really changed? Was she really—out of her mind, and was she, Lindy, the only one who could not see it?

'Promise,' repeated Arran, pressing her fingers into Lindy's arm.

Suddenly Lindy's resistance collapsed. She felt faint, and the height at which they were standing increased her dizziness. All she wanted was to get away, back to ground level, away from this nightmare. What did it matter? John was no longer hers to renounce, and never would be. Let Arran have her way.

'Very well,' she said, 'I promise.' She burst into a flood of tears.

Arran watched her stonily, and made no attempt to comfort her.

The night was dark and still. The three women sat in the drawing-room. The light flickering of the fire, and the occasional fall of a coal, were the only sounds inside. Lindy sewed busily, Arran was reading, Mary Dazill sat as usual with folded hands. None of them had spoken for over an hour. There was no more music, now, in the evenings; the piano had been closed since Leonard's death. They were waiting for Ralph de Boulter's return.

'The train's very late,' said Lindy at last. 'I heard the dog-cart leave an hour ago.' Nobody answered. 'Of course it often is,' she added, looking from one to the other of her companions. 'Especially in winter. Or perhaps the time has been changed.—Arran, dear, it's time you went to bed, you know.'

Arran seemed to have been waiting for the word of release. She closed her book, and with a murmured good night, hurried away.

Lindy folded up her work. As usual, the presence of Mary Dazill troubled her. Her cheeks burned, the thoughts raced through her mind. If only she could have found relief in speech! If only she could have begun and said: 'We were happy before you came. Why don't you go away?'

But no words came. The silence seemed more intense than ever. Mary Dazill sat motionless, as if unaware of Lindy's presence. She was not even ignoring Lindy—she was lost in her own thoughts. Ah, what could they be?

Lindy rose. 'Will you wait up for my father?' she said timidly. 'If he wants me when he comes in, you have only to call.'

'Yes, I will wait for him,' said Mary Dazill.

Lindy said 'Good night,' and hurried away.

Next morning early, there was a thundering on the front door. In the drive, lanterns moved, and there was a confusion of men's voices, a sound of horses' hooves, the undoing of bolts and chains. Then there were cries of women, and footsteps running along the corridors. Lindy woke to see Mary Dazill bending over her. She sat up quickly.

'Lindy,' said Mary Dazill, 'you must prepare yourself for a shock. Something terrible has happened.'

'Arran!' gasped Lindy. Her thoughts flew at once to the high turret, and instantly she saw Arran's body lying in a still heap below.

'No, not Arran,' said Mary. 'Your father. He is dead. They found the horse and trap in the drive this morning. And your father and the groom were found further back, lying in the road. The groom was unconscious—but your father—'

Lindy stared and stared. Then she began to laugh wildly. Mary Dazill bit her lip and went away.

I I

The death of Ralph de Boulter caused a great stir in the countryside: it came so soon after the death of his son, and so soon before
his proposed marriage—for it was revealed at the inquest that he
had already arranged for the banns to be called. The only witness
to the cause of death was Baxter, the groom: and even he could
scarcely be called a witness. He himself had been thrown out of the
dog-cart when the accident happened, and he remembered nothing
more. Still, the story he told was sufficient to confirm the verdict.

He said that, according to his master's orders, passed on to him
by Miss Lindy, he had driven the dog-cart to the station, to meet
the train due in at twenty minutes past nine. The train was a little
late, ten minutes perhaps, not more. Mr. de Boulter duly arrived.

'Did anyone else alight from the train?' said the Coroner.

'Yes,' said Baxter, 'one or two villagers.' He did not know what
happened to them, as Mr. de Boulter appeared at once and got into
the trap; but they probably crossed the bridge and went off on the
other road, since no one passed the scene of the accident till the
following morning.

Well, said the Coroner, 'so Mr. de Boulter joined you, at about
half-past nine. What happened then? You drove off, with him
beside you?'

'No, sir,' corrected Baxter. 'Mr. de Boulter took the reins. He
always did. I never drove the dog-cart except when I was sent to
meet him. I gave him the reins, and *he* drove off.'

'At a great pace, I suppose?' said the Coroner. 'Mr. de Boulter
was a fast driver, was he not?'

'He was, sir, as a rule,' said Baxter. 'But not on this occasion.
He took the reins, as a matter of habit, and the whip was in its

socket beside him, but so far as I remember, he never used it. He seemed tired, or as if he had something on his mind, and for the first quarter of a mile we went quite slowly. Of course, sir, if you want my opinion, Mr. de Boulter hasn't been at all himself lately—'

The Coroner checked him. 'No, no, my good man:—no surmises. Tell us the facts, please.'

Baxter continued: The pony, however, finding her master's hand so unexpectedly slack, had suddenly decided to make her own pace; she had been idle for several days, during Mr. de Boulter's absence; and she was therefore full of oats, and frisky; it wasn't long before they were bounding along the road at a spanking pace.

'The night was dark, I believe?' interrupted the Coroner. 'I believe you said that there was no moon when you drove to the station?'

'No, sir,' said Baxter. 'I mean—there was no moon when I drove to the station, and it was very dark then. But when we drove back, the moon was rising. It was a full moon, very big and yellow; and we could see the road quite clearly.' He went on to say, however, that this had not made for greater safety, because the pony, now that she could see, was able to go faster; and yet because of the trees at the side of the road, the shadows were very confusing; and in fact she was inclined to shy at them. The night was cold, but windless—at least, there was not enough wind to stir the branches.

'So you were going at a good pace; and Mr. de Boulter was letting the pony have her head. Now to come to the accident. Try to remember the details, as far as you can. Where did it occur?'

'Just about five hundred yards before you get to the big gates,' said Baxter, wondering why he had to answer such silly questions. 'That was why they didn't find us before, maybe. You turn off the main road, you see, down the lane; and nobody hardly comes that way, unless they're coming to Chetwode Lodge by the main entrance. It's the loneliest spot of all.'

'Now,' the Coroner leaned forward, folding his hands, 'tell us just what occurred.'

Baxter took a deep breath. Yes, that was it: just what *had* occurred? One moment they had been bowling along the lane, expecting in a moment to swing to the left through the wrought-iron gates of the drive; and the next moment—

'Well, sir,' said Baxter, 'it all happened so sudden. It was as if Mr. de Boulter was suddenly struck by a thunderbolt—'

'One moment,' said the Coroner sharply. 'Do you mean that? There was no thunderstorm, was there? The night was calm, you said?'

'No, no,' said Baxter unhappily. 'I didn't mean that. I meant just, it was so sudden. He fell forward, as if he'd been struck—and the pony swerved towards the trees. I tried to grab the reins—but I couldn't: the next thing I knew, the dog-cart struck a tree; I heard the smashing of wood; we were both thrown out, and that's all I know, sir. I fell out sideways, as it were, but Mr. de Boulter must have been thrown out frontwards and bashed his head against the tree, for I heard afterwards, when I came to, how his head was all smashed in—'

The Coroner checked him again, this time with a smile. 'After that,' he reminded him, 'your mind became a blank. You recovered consciousness eighteen hours later, in your own home; and you may thank God for your own preservation. Very well, Baxter— you may go.'

Medical evidence was given; and the evidence of the labourer from the village who found the two men lying in the road, and roused the gardener. The pony was quietly grazing along the edge of the drive, dragging the damaged dog-cart behind her. The village doctor assured the Coroner that Mr. de Boulter's injuries must have resulted in instantaneous death. But it was not against a tree that he had bashed out his brains: there was no trace of blood on the trunk of the great elm tree against which the trap had been shattered. There was, however, a large jagged stone near by, which would account for the damage.

So a verdict of 'Accidental death' was recorded; and the village settled down to watch the strange new situation now developing under their eyes at Chetwode Lodge. What would be the next sensation? These things always run in threes, they said, as they trampled the grass round the new-made grave, and turned over the mourning-cards attached to the wreaths, now withering in piles. The one from Lindy and Arran was in ink, in Lindy's bold handwriting; the card was yellowing fast, and the ink was fading from black to brown. But the wreath from Mary Dazill carried only a visiting-card, not even edged with black, carrying no words of love or sorrow: merely a visiting-card engraved with her name. It was callous, all agreed; but they were also agreed that anything written would have been unseemly. Yet what could be more unseemly, in the present circumstances, than her being there at all? The village tea-tables rocked with scandal: and pity for the bereaved daughters overflowed.

Book III

I

'Well!' said Mrs. Barratt, 'you can imagine with what curiosity everybody in the neighbourhood wanted to see what would happen next. Ralph de Boulter's will was the focal point of attention; all sorts of rumours flew around before its provisions became known. Some said that he had left all his money to Mary Dazill absolutely, others that his children were to share it with her only on condition that they all three lived on in that house; and many other strange conditions were invented and ascribed to Ralph's infatuated brain. Naturally it struck everyone as very strange that this terrible accident should have happened so soon after his journey to London for the expressed purpose of rearranging his affairs; and some darkly hinted that there must be some connection between the two happenings. By now, the facts about Mary Dazill's mother were known, and people began to look at her askance—or they would have done, if ever she had allowed herself to be seen. Her mother a murderess! Two deaths in the house, during her first year there! There must be some connection. They worked hard to find or invent one. And if it had turned out that Ralph had left his money to Mary Dazill, life would have been made very unpleasant for her.

'But, of course, he had not. He had never thought to die before his marriage, and all his provision for Mary had depended on her becoming his wife. So the whole of his property—as Leonard was dead—was divided between Lindy and Arran. It seemed, however, that he had already transferred to Mary, as a birthday gift, some shares in a Burmese ruby mine, the income from which was meant to be pin-money for her before her marriage to him. This was now all she had to live on.'

There was a pause. 'Poor girl!' said Fitzbrown. 'So Lindy and Arran were mistresses of the situation. She had to leave, I suppose?'

'No,' said Mrs. Barratt, "strangely enough, no. Of course, everyone thought that Lindy would lose no time at all in getting rid of her. But that wasn't how it turned out. When all the people concerned with the funeral had gone away, and the excitement was over, it was found that Mary Dazill was still there. Arran had been sent away, to stay with relatives: the doctor said that he would not be responsible for her sanity if she stayed in that house of disasters. Lindy had wished to go with her; but the doctor had advised a complete change, of persons as well as scene.

'So Mary Dazill, and Lindy, by now her mortal enemy, were left alone together in that great house, to settle their quarrel as best they could.'

'But,' said Fitzbrown, 'you still haven't explained why Mary Dazill didn't go.'

'Ah,' said Mrs. Barratt, 'as to that, I don't know. Because she didn't wish to, I suppose...'

Winter was long in passing that year. Now it was the beginning of April, yet still the cold winds blew from the east, withering grass and plants and trees. Lindy stood in her turret window, looking out over the lawns, wondering how all this would end. She seemed, now, to be always watching from a distance, those two figures retreating. Why could she not take a strong line? People had always called her strong. Her face had character, they said: she looked like one made to protect the weak. Why then, couldn't she say, as friends like Lucy advised, 'I wish you to leave here. Please make arrangements and go?'

No, it was useless: she could not. From the moment that Mary Dazill had entered the house, she had held them all hypnotised, by love or by fear. Those who loved her, she destroyed; those who hated her, she seemed to paralyse, to rob of their will-power, even of their speech. Yet she obsessed Lindy's thoughts, whether she was present or absent. In her presence, Lindy's cheeks burned, her words faltered, her movements were jerky. In her absence Lindy thought of nothing else. Leonard was nothing but a dim memory to her now; her father, though more vivid, was a loss which she thought of with amazement but without grief, though she had believed she loved him. Arran—she impatiently brushed aside the thought of Arran, for she could not have borne ill-health, mental or physical, at the moment, and all her tender sympathy was exhausted: she was glad Arran was no longer there, to watch her and discover the strange hardness of her heart. As for John, now for ever at Mary Dazill's side, she could not remember what it was like to love, to look forward to a life of normal happiness and normal cares: he seemed to her utterly unreal, and her only response to his now obviously flaunted devotion was a shrug of contempt. But Mary Dazill—ah, Mary Dazill!—was it not the truth that far from telling her to go, Lindy would have used every means to prevent her? Lucy had said, in that irritating dogmatic way of hers, 'If I were in your

place, I would have her luggage packed and sent to the station.'
Poor, foolish, interfering Lucy! Did she not see that Lindy, if she
had come in one day and found Mary Dazill's luggage packed and
waiting in the hall, would have been utterly dismayed?

Oh, no, Mary Dazill was not to escape so lightly. The time would
come when, with all her indifference, her coldness, she would pay
for having broken Lindy's pride, her spirit as well as her heart.
Lindy's chance would come, if she could keep her enemy there
within her reach, and yet contrive to show no sign.

But what Lindy failed to realise was, she had no need to scheme;
for Mary Dazill had no thought of leaving. It mattered nothing to
her whether she lived among friends or foes; all she desired was
to stay here, where once a ray of sunshine, however brief and
deceptive, had warmed her, and never to have to face the strange,
brutal outer world again. For this harbourage, the daily presence
of Lindy's hostility seemed to her a little price to pay.

2

Mary Dazill walked, with John beside her, along the river-path.
The water flowed rippling over the stones: it would have been
easy to wade across to the island, for the long drought had left the
river fordable, as it seldom was in winter; but now there was ice at
its edges, and the tall grasses of the island lay bowed and yellow
before the withering gales. Every morning she walked here, and
John came with her. He had said, the first time: 'May I join you?'
and she had answered indifferently: 'I can't prevent you, if you
choose.' Her silence—for she never spoke unless he addressed
her—would have daunted a less persistent lover; yet he came.

The wind howled in the tops of the pines. Mary Dazill stopped, as she always did, to look across at the island. They stood there for a long time without speaking, while the bitter wind lashed their faces. Suddenly John said:

'You want to go across there, don't you?'

Mary Dazill turned to look at him in surprise. 'Sometimes I do,' she said quietly.

'Let me take you,' he said eagerly. 'Look how shallow the river is to-day. I can carry you. I promise I won't—hurt you. I'd do anything for you, Mary, you know.'

A faint smile stirred her lips as she still studied him curiously. 'Why should you?'

He gazed at her without speaking.

'You know,' she went on, 'why I want to go there?'

'Yes, I know.'

'And yet you want to take me?'

'I'd do anything for you,' he repeated. 'I've proved that, haven't I?'

They wound their way down the black, slippery bank to the water's edge. He lifted her carefully, and waded into the stream. The icy, numbing water rippled round his ankles, and the round pebbles rolled from under his feet; but he strode along without stumbling, and her weight seemed nothing to him. He placed her carefully, like a precious china ornament, on her feet on the other side. She did not thank him. She turned away, and made for the upper point of the island; and for a long time she stood there, as if on the prow of a ship, gazing upstream.

At last he said: 'You must come away now, Mary. If you stand there any longer in this wind, you'll catch cold.'

She turned and looked down at him where he sat on a rock a

little below. 'No,' she said, 'I'm not coming back yet. You must go, though.'

'But, Mary, you can't get back alone!'

'Oh, yes I can, perfectly well. The river is quite shallow, as you said yourself just now. I want you to leave me alone here, please.' Her voice had taken on a sharper quality, a quality which formerly he had feared as a dog fears the whip-lash. He rose, and came towards her.

'Mary,' he said, 'this has got to end.'

She stared at him without understanding. He gripped her wrist.

'You have played with me long enough,' he said. 'Why do you think I've let you lead me about like this, as if I were your slave? Do you think I'm going to wait for ever?'

He held her wrist lightly. She was obliged to listen, though she tried to turn away. He went on, more and more violently:

'I've given up everything for you—Lindy, my career, my friends, even my people. You don't know what I've been through— what I'm going through now, because of you. There's hardly a soul, either in my home or out of it, who'll speak to me. They're convinced I've gone to the devil.' He laughed. 'They're quite right. But they don't know what my game is—and that it's worth the candle.'

He gazed up at her eagerly, as if he expected her to agree with him. She said at last:

'I'm sorry, John. I shouldn't have let you come with me. But I thought it would be too unkind to keep sending you away—and I'm a little tired of hurting people.'

He did not seem to hear. 'You will marry me—you must. Don't worry about my family: they'll get over it. And if it's money you're thinking of—I have some of my own, you know, enough for us to live on. You need someone to look after you. There's nothing to prevent you, now that—now that you're free.'

Mary Dazill turned away. 'Free!' was all she said.

He hurried on. 'Of course I know you were in love with Leonard, for a while—after you got engaged to his father. You couldn't help all that. But you know he was cheating you, don't you? Why, he told even *me* what he'd do—how he'd prove—'

He glanced up at her; and there was something in her face that checked him. 'Mary,' he said, 'if you don't marry me, I'll shoot myself. I swear it.'

At that, she turned back to him with almost a smile. 'Don't do that,' she said. 'If you do, people will say I am responsible. They may even say I shot you myself. I believe there are people who say I killed Leonard—Lucy Brown, for instance, and Lindy and Arran, and all the people they've told; perhaps even you.'

'No, no,' said John. 'not I.'

'Why not?' said Mary Dazill. 'After all, my mother was a murderess... Now will you please go?'

John left her, standing on the highest point of the island, in the piercing wind. When he had waded across the shallow water and reached the bank, he turned to look at her. Then he slunk away.

3

Lucy sat in the drawing-room. She had not taken off her hat and coat, and her shopping-basket loaded with provisions stood beside her chair. When Lindy entered, she half rose, for she had thought for a moment that it was a stranger. Lindy was dressed severely, like a nurse; and her whole manner breathed competence.

'Oh, Lindy!' said Lucy. 'Is it true? Is it really serious?'

'Yes,' said Lindy crisply, 'very serious. Double pneumonia. And the doctor says her heart is weak.'

'Oh dear, how terrible for you!' Lucy was all compassion for Lindy. 'How did it happen? I heard to-day for the first time, or I would have been here before.'

'I don't know,' said Lindy. 'I think she had been out walking by the river, and caught a chill. Her shoes and stockings were wet.'

'And you have to nurse her? Oh, my dear, what retribution! How she must feel it, after all the suffering she has caused you.'

'She doesn't,' said Lindy bluntly. 'She feels nothing. She's too ill.'

Lucy's eyes opened wide. 'You can bring yourself to—You must be glad poor Arran isn't here.'

'I am,' said Lindy.

'But you'll get ill yourself, if you don't have help. Shall I come in and sit with her one evening, so that you can get some rest?' Her voice was somewhat faltering; it was clear that this time she felt no enthusiasm for the work of mercy. She and Lindy seemed suddenly to have become strangers, looking at each other coldly across a deep ravine.

'No, thank you,' said Lindy. 'I can manage quite well. I look after her during the day, and we have a woman from the village coming in at night. I assure you, the doctor is quite satisfied.'

Lucy was aware of the sharp note in her voice. She gathered herself together, and picked up the basket.

'You know best,' she said. 'I hope—I hope you will have your reward.'

A week later, Mary Dazill died.

4

'So Mary Dazill died,' said Mrs. Barratt. 'And on the whole, it was agreed that this was best. She was buried, as you know, in a distant corner of the churchyard. I never heard that any relative came to her funeral, or ever visited her grave.

'Lindy became the mistress of Chetwode Lodge; and after a while, Arran rejoined her. She seemed to be quite cured. And so they lived on there together. My mother, soon afterwards, met my father and became engaged to him; and then came her marriage, which took her to a neighbouring village. So she saw very little of the two sisters. And in fact, for years they hardly left the house and grounds, except to go to church and to the graveyard. As years passed, and people in the village who knew their story either died, or went away, or forgot, they began to emerge a little more; and there were, and still are, occasional tea-parties, and in the summer, garden-parties at the Lodge.' She laughed. 'I assure you, an invitation from the Misses de Boulter is a command.'

'They give very generously to our good causes,' deprecated the Vicar.

Mrs. Barratt pushed her knitting-needles into the ball of wool. 'Well,' she said, 'that's the end of the story. It's rather unsatisfactory, I'm afraid, because one can't know what happened. My mother, as I told you, never believed that Leonard's death was suicide; but even she couldn't maintain that Mr. de Boulter was not accidentally killed, strange though it seemed, following so closely on the others; and as for Mary Dazill—'

'Well, Mallett,' said the Vicar cheerfully, as Mallett rose, 'have you a theory? Or is it all moonshine?'

Mallett shook his head. 'Poor girl!' he said.

The Vicar was about to ask him another question, when Dr. Fitzbrown interrupted:

But you haven't told us what happened to young Despenser,' he said to Mrs. Barratt. 'How did *he* take Mary Dazill's death?'

That, too, I m afraid I can't tell you,' she answered. There's no means of knowing. But he certainly never came back to marry Lindy. My mother said he was commonly believed to have gone abroad, and died there. Some said he had become a missionary, others that he went to work in a leper colony. But no one was certain, nor whether it was to China or Africa or some distant island in the Pacific he had gone. His family left this neighbourhood, and so there was no means of knowing.'

Epilogue

I

It was a year later, once again a soft rainy evening in November. In the Vicarage sitting-room, Dr. Fitzbrown and Superintendent Mallett sat playing bridge with the Vicar and his wife. The strange story they had pondered over together had forged a bond between them; and though nowadays they seldom spoke of it, it was the unseen basis of their friendship. This cosy room, smelling of dust and tobacco-smoke, was a little oasis of human companionship; but outside lay the lonely graveyard, and its memories, prowling round, wanting to get into the circle, the charmed circle of light and life… Thoughts like these, hardly expressible in words, sometimes flitted across Fitzbrown's mind, and gave an added value to the solid, cheerful company of his friends.

'Yes,' said the Vicar, shaking his head as Mallett stacked the cards and began dealing, 'I'm afraid poor Miss Arran is sinking fast. I doubt if she'll last the week out.'

'H'm,' said Mallett. 'What's wrong?'

'Pneumonia, I'm afraid,' said the Vicar. And her heart is very, very weak.' Fitzbrown glanced up sharply. The Vicar continued: 'At her age, you know—'

'How is Lindy taking it?' said Mrs. Barratt. 'I called there this morning, but she sent a message to say she couldn't see me. Poor thing! They've always been so very devoted. Lindy won't know what to do without her, though she's always been the strong-minded one.' She picked up her hand, and began studying it. 'Did *you* see her, dear?'

'Yes, I saw her,' said Mr. Barratt, 'this afternoon. She let me see Arran for a moment, too. But I don't think Arran knew me. She has become—how shall I put it?—a little childish in her mind, during the past year. She has always been the placid one. But now, her thoughts seem to have left this world altogether. She simply lay there with her eyes wide open, smiling, and obviously unaware of the present.'

'I wonder what she thinks of,' said Fitzbrown.

It was nearly eleven o'clock. The last rubber was finishing. The fire was showing more grey ash than red glow; but the room was warm, and heavy with pipe-smoke; and the bridge-players were absorbed. When the telephone-bell shrilled out on the Vicar's desk, everybody started. The Vicar leaned backwards in his chair and picked up the receiver:

'Hullo, yes?' he said irritably. Then, as he listened, his head craned forward, and his voice changed. 'Yes, all right, very well, I'll be there immediately.' He dropped the receiver back, and stared round at the circle.

'It's Miss de Boulter's chauffeur,' he said. 'He says Miss Arran is taken suddenly worse, and they've been trying to get hold of their own doctor from Broxeter, but he happens to be out. Do I know of anyone else nearer at hand?'

They all gazed at Fitzbrown.

'It's providential,' said Mrs. Barratt.

'Better have a drink, Dudley, my boy,' said Mallett with a grin.

'I'll start the car,' said Fitzbrown.

'No,' said the Vicar, 'the car is coming round to fetch us. She wants me to be there as well, it seems. Actually we could walk there in five minutes by the lane; and it takes just as long if not longer to be driven round the front way. But everything connected with the Misses de Boulter has to be done with due ceremony—even dying.'

A few minutes later, there was a sound of the car turning outside, and the beam from the headlamps flashed across the windows.

'You'll stay here, Superintendent?' said Mrs. Barratt.

'I'm afraid I shall have to,' said Mallett, 'if you can put up with me. I came over in Fitzbrown's car. But I don't suppose you'll be long?'

The house-bell rang. The Vicar hurried out.

'No, of course not,' said Fitzbrown, following him.

Mrs. Barratt glanced at her remaining guest. 'Another glass of whisky, Superintendent?'

'Thank you, ma'am,' said Mallett. 'And what about a hand of cribbage? Seems quite in keeping, doesn't it?'

Mrs. Barratt began building up the fire.

2

It was three o'clock next morning when they returned. Mrs. Barratt had gone to bed. Mallett lay with his feet on another chair and a newspaper over his face, quietly snoring. Outside in the lane, the big black limousine crawled up softly, and released its two passengers, pale, haggard and weary.

Mrs. Barratt appeared at the head of the stairs.

'Is it all over?' she whispered.

The Vicar nodded. 'Come down, my dear, will you? We've got something to tell you.'

Mallett woke with a start, and emerged blinking from under the newspaper. 'What is it?' he said.

'The sequel to the story,' said Fitzbrown.

As formerly they had gathered round Mrs. Barratt, so now they turned to Fitzbrown.

'When we arrived,' he began, 'we were shown into a large room—the drawing-room, I suppose—with no fire. Here we sat for a very long time, in our coats—and nothing happened at all. I had been expecting to be called up at once to see the patient—but the whole house was silent, and when I went to the door, I could hear nothing. I had no idea where to go to look for anyone. In any ordinary house, if it were a patient of mine, I would just walk upstairs and find the room for myself; but in this house, so large and dark—there was no light in the hall or on the stairs—and apparently so empty, I didn't feel justified in wandering about unattended, especially as my visit was not really authorised.'

'*You* knew your way about, James,' said Mrs. Barratt. 'You could have taken him.'

'Yes, yes, my dear,' said the Vicar apologetically, 'but I can't tell you what a strange feeling came over us as we sat there—a feeling that something was going on into which we mustn't intrude. And, of course, we expected to be called at any moment.'

Fitzbrown took up the tale again. 'Well, at last, just as we were thinking of leaving, we heard sounds: first, feet running overhead, then voices. Then the door opened, and—'

'Miss de Boulter appeared,' interrupted the Vicar. 'She stood there in the doorway. You know how tall and straight she is, my dear. Her hair is very white, but her eyebrows are still black, and it gives her a most commanding look. She was as white as paper. She stood there quite stiffly, but I could see that she was swaying a little. Fitzbrown hurried towards her—'

'I said, "Where is she?"' continued Fitzbrown. '"I'm a doctor." She looked at me dully and said, "It's too late. My sister's dead."'

'I led her to a chair,' said the Vicar. 'She didn't actually faint, though she stayed with her eyes shut for a little while. Fitzbrown gave her something to smell, and that seemed to revive her. Then she said, "Vicar, I want to speak to you alone."

'I said, "Speak on, Miss Lindy—don't be afraid. This young man here is a doctor—and besides, he knows your story." After that, she took no more notice of Fitzbrown. She talked to me, and he sat in the background. We've been all this time hearing what poor Lindy had to say. At first it seemed disconnected. Then I gradually began to see the object of it. It was something like this:

'"Why didn't she tell me, instead of keeping it to herself all these years! I believed I knew her every thought. She did it to spare me, she said. But then, of course, I deceived her, too—I never thought her poor brain could stand the weight of such a secret. I didn't know she could carry almost to the grave a secret of her own. I see now—I see it all! When we all thought she was going out of her mind—and so she was, but none of us knew why. Oh, Arran, Arran, why didn't you tell me? I could have borne it then. I was young—I would have recovered. But now, when my time is so short—how can I bear the thoughts I'm faced with now?"'

'I tried to recall her,' said the Vicar. 'Her despair was terrible. The words came quickly, and her eyes—which are still dark and fine—were filled with what I can only describe as torment. I asked her, as gently as I could, "Tell me what is troubling you. God is merciful. It's never too late to seek forgiveness." But she went on, as if not hearing, or not understanding:

'"She came here, and we thought she was the destroyer. But she herself was destroyed. I thought it just. I thought I had the right. Look what she had done to me, and mine! I thought, if she hadn't actually killed them, it was through her that they died. She took them all, and destroyed them. So in the end, I destroyed her."'

The Vicar looked round at his hearers. 'I said, "Miss Lindy, do you know what you are saying? Are you trying to tell me that you are responsible for the death of a human being—a human being at your mercy, in your power, entrusted to your care?"'

'She turned then, and looked at me quite calmly, almost contemptuously: "Yes," she said. "That is what I am telling you. Don't look so frightened, you foolish man. I tell you because you are the only person I can tell. I must tell someone. After all, if I could keep such a secret to myself for fifty years, surely you can do so for the few years of life that remain to me? Not that I ask you to promise anything: tell anyone you please. I am indifferent. No one will trouble to punish an old woman like me." She gave a strange laugh. "It could not be proved, in any case, after so many years."

'I was shocked, I must confess, to see her so hardhearted. Then Fitzbrown came forward, out of the shadows. He said: "Do you mean you killed Mary Dazill?"'

Fitzbrown interrupted: 'She turned and looked at me then,' he said, 'and I admit it sent a strange shiver down my spine. But I looked her full in the eyes—very fine dark eyes they are too, as the Vicar says. She answered me, looking me up and down: "You are a doctor?" "Yes," I said. "Then perhaps you can answer your own question."

'I said: "I don't know what you mean."

'She said: "You have just asked me, did I kill Mary Dazill? And I say to you, did I? Suppose you had a patient, seriously ill—"

'"Double pneumonia," I put in.

'"Yes," she said, "double pneumonia, through no one's fault but her own."

'"I don't know about that," I said; but she continued:

'"And suppose you had a nurse, who nursed that patient assiduously night and day—or appeared to, in so far as she never left her. You might, of course, look at it in another way and call it mounting guard. But I suppose that had never occurred to you. No, and it didn't occur to your colleague, either."

'"But what did you do?" I said. "Did you poison her?"

'"No," she said: "No. That was not possible to me. It wasn't in my nature or my upbringing to do anything violent. Besides, it was not necessary. I merely—disobeyed the doctor's orders. He said that careful nursing would be required if she was to survive. I stayed beside her—but I did not nurse her. I did none of the things he told me to do. As for his medicines, I poured them out, dose by dose—and threw them away. There was a medicine for the heart, I remember—digitalis, isn't it? Her heart was very weak, he said. I gave her none of it. When he found that it was having no effect, he decided that she was beyond help. He called it 'failing to respond to treatment.'"

'"You took a great risk," I said. "What if she had over recovered sufficiently to tell him what you were doing? I take it she was too weak, most of the time. But people do often recover strength suddenly, especially when they are dying."

'"Yes," she said. "That's true. My sister was dying, yet she found strength to tell me—But I knew that Mary Dazill would not tell. She did not care. She no longer wanted to live. I thought at the time, it was because she knew she deserved to die."'

'There was a long silence,' said the Vicar. 'Fitzbrown went back to his place again, and she remained brooding. At last I ventured to ask her: "Miss Lindy, what has made you change your mind?"

'She turned and looked at me for so long that I wondered if she had decided not to speak. Then she stood up. "Come with me," she said.

'We followed her, up the wide staircase, along the corridor. Times have changed since her father's day: these great old houses can't be kept up as they used to be. But I was shocked to see how everything had fallen into decay. Downstairs, they kept up a pretty good show of riches; but up here, on the first floor, the walls were showing signs of damp, and what had once been a magnificent cherry-red carpet was riddled with moth-channels. The gilt fittings were tarnished, mirrors were spotted with mould; the damp chill of an inadequately-heated mansion struck home.

'She brought us to the room where Arran lay. Fitzbrown examined her: the body was still warm, but she was dead, peacefully smiling, as the newly-dead so often are.

'"She lies there and smiles," we heard Lindy saying bitterly. "She has left me to carry this burden alone. She has dropped it at last."

'Fitzbrown mechanically picked up the bottle of medicine on the bedside table and looked at it. Lindy smiled wryly: "Ah, no, doctor, you need not suspect me of having neglected *her*. I would have given my life to have been allowed to take her place. I carried out every order. I nursed her night and day. But this time, it was unsuccessful."

'Then she led us out of the room, and closed the door softly. We followed her, back along the corridor, into the hall. It seemed as if we had heard all she was willing to tell us. I was preparing to take my leave, but Fitzbrown suddenly burst out with: "But, Miss Lindy— what made you change your mind—about Mary Dazill, I mean?"

'I was afraid for the effect of this on her. But she seemed to have accepted him as a friend, or at least as confessor, instead of myself. She gave him a long appraising look: then she actually smiled. I could see she had taken a fancy to him. In a minute, we were all back in the drawing-room again; but this time, it was I who sat in the background. She told the rest of the story to Fitzbrown; and now, she was no longer incoherent. She told it quietly. She said—but you had better tell it yourself, Fitzbrown.'

3

Fitzbrown said: 'I asked her many questions—all that I wanted to. She seemed, now, quite ready to answer. She didn't treat me like a stranger. I said to her: "Why did you hate Mary Dazill so much? Did *you* think she shot your brother?"

'She showed no surprise at my knowing her story. She said: "No. I never believed those silly stories. In spite of all the nonsense Lucy talked, I always believed he shot himself. He was quite capable of it. I believed he was in love with Mary Dazill. He shot himself—so I thought—because he wasn't worthy of her. Lucy was in love with him herself: how could *she* know—a silly little girl like her—what people like Leonard think and feel? He was utterly elusive—none of us was fine enough to understand him—except perhaps Mary Dazill."

"'And the arrow? You remember the arrow Lucy Brown said someone shot at her in the dark?'"

"'I thought she invented it. These matter-of-fact people—they are the most credulous of all, when something disturbs them.'"

"'You never thought your father might have been responsible?'"

"'Yes,' said Lindy, 'I did think of that. He was a violent man. If he thought that Leonard was deceiving him—or was his rival, even by accident—he might easily have killed him. But I dismissed that too. To me Mary Dazill was his real destroyer, no matter whose hand fired the shot. That one fact made me almost indifferent to the truth. Still, in my heart I always believed it was suicide.'"

"'And your father? You never had any reason to think that his death was anything but a pure accident?'"

"'No,' she said, 'no,' but I could see that the question no longer interested her. She was gazing beyond me, answering automatically. It was cold and damp in this room. I remember noticing the grand piano and thinking that this atmosphere wouldn't be good for it. I wondered what it would sound like, now, after all the years since Leonard had sat there playing it, on the last night of his life, while Lucy Brown watched him from the shadows... Miss Lindy didn't seem to notice the cold. She sat bolt upright in her gilt-legged chair. Round her neck was a fine gold chain, carrying a locket. I wondered if she still had John Despenser's picture inside. I watched her, and saw that her lips were moving. At first the words were inaudible: then I could hear them, though she spoke softly:

"'Yes—yes. I did: I bore her a grudge because of it. I thought it was not fair of her to have asked it of me. I gave it—but I grudged it." She turned to me as if for an appreciation of her point of view.

"'Grudged what, Miss Lindy?' I asked her. "What was it you gave her? You mean Mary Dazill, don't you?'"

'She frowned impatiently. "No, no—my sister. I did not think it fair that she should ask me for such a promise. I knew she loved him—but to my mind, that was the very reason why she should not have asked it."

"'Asked you to promise not to marry him, you mean?'"

"I was a little impatient of her weakness, too. Each time she cried, or fainted, or failed to face our difficulties, I thought, 'Where would we be if *I* were weak, like you?' I was prepared to do any-thing—to sacrifice my own happiness—for her; and she couldn't even see him and say a few conventional words! I have always despised weakness." She gave a little laugh. "Arran, weak! If only you hadn't been so strong!"

'At that, an odd doubt crossed my mind. "Miss Lindy," I said, "you don't mean that *Arran* had anything to do with the shooting of Leonard? After all, she did go back there—they *did* find her looking for that book, behind the desk in his room—and she was terribly upset when you discovered her there. She was ill for long afterwards, wasn't she?" I became quite excited. "That might account for all her queer behaviour, subsequently—especially if she thought that you all suspected her. She might even have shot the arrow at Lucy, when she found out that Lucy was playing the amateur detective. But why—why should she kill her brother? There's no motive that I can see..."

'I don't suppose Miss Lindy heard a word of all this. She waited until I finished talking. Perhaps she had continued her own con-versation with herself, without reference to me, as I had continued mine. At any rate, I heard her say:

"'John—John.'"

'Her eyes grew big with terror again. She covered her face with her hands, and for the first time, she shuddered. At that, the Vicar, realising that something had changed, came back to her and laid a hand on her shoulder.'

The Vicar resumed: 'Yes, I laid a hand on her shoulder. I said, "Miss Lindy, tell us: was that what your sister told you just now, before she died?—that it was John Despenser who shot your brother? Don't be afraid to speak. He has been dead now for many a long year. John Despenser shot him, and your sister saw him—isn't that so?"

'There was no answer. She sat there with her face buried in her hands. We could say and do nothing more. And so we left her. To-day I shall go back again. But unless she makes some sign, I shall pretend that nothing has occurred.'

4

'John Despenser!' whispered Mrs. Barratt. 'So it was he after all—the one whom nobody ever dreamed of suspecting.'

'Pardon me,' Mallett rumbled from his chair. 'I suspected him, all along.'

'Pooh!' said Fitzbrown. 'That's easy to say—now. You're exactly like the people who read detective stories: you suspect all the people concerned, and when the guilt is plain, you say, "I was right after all."'

'Quite right, my boy,' conceded Mallett. 'I certainly didn't pick out John Despenser—there wasn't enough evidence, at this time of day, for that.'

'It wasn't fair, I suppose,' jeered Fitzbrown.

'But,' continued Mallett imperturbably, 'I differed from the rest of you in one respect: although I suspected, at different times, the father, Lindy, Arran, Mary Dazill and even Lucy, I did not forget to think about John, the moment he disappeared from sight out of the story. And, therefore, I dare say I could build up the case against him better than any of you. For instance, I noticed that he was present when Lucy announced her discovery—and that he was in the house on that night when she made her headlong rush down the avenue. Doubtless he knew better than anyone how easy it would be to shoot an arrow from Leonard's study—where the bows and arrows were kept—across the terrace to the avenue. I also noticed that he was there when Lucy announced her intention to drop the matter—of course, actually, like the rest of you, I thought it was suicide. But Lucy—beg pardon, ma'am, your lady mother—was right after all.'

Mrs. Barratt sighed. 'So Arran saw him! What a terrible thing for the poor girl! That accounts for all her behaviour—her collapse—her horror of John whenever he came near her. And—and, of course, *that* was why she made Lindy promise never to marry him! It was not selfishness at all. And when you think how she herself had loved John, and been deceived by him—I suppose she loved him still, and couldn't give him away. The utmost she could do was to save Lindy from him.'

Fitzbrown brushed aside this aspect. He leaned across to Mallett, who showed signs of going to sleep again.

'But look here, Mallett!' he said. 'How do you account for the death of the father? I suppose one should always suspect foul play—but it's difficult to see what Despenser can have to do with that.'

Mallett roused himself. 'Oh, I don't know,' he said somnolently. 'Ralph de Boulter went to see Despenser's parents, didn't he,

before he left for London? He went to tell them of his proposals
for the marriage-settlement on his daughter Lindy—that is to say,
to tie the young man up once and for all. The motive for all this,
I take it, was Despenser's passion for Mary Dazill—that was why
he shot Leonard. He saw, or thought he saw, that Leonard had
double-crossed him. He knew—just because of his jealousy—jealousy gives keen perceptions—that, whatever Leonard intended,
he would inevitably fall in love with her, if he had not done so
already—and that she was in love with Leonard. One crime leads
to another. If, after all, she married Ralph de Boulter, the first crime
was wasted: he had murdered his friend for nothing. If he got rid
of de Boulter, he saved himself from Lindy's clutches, as well as
destroying Mary's future husband. He must have heard, when
de Boulter visited them, what time he would be returning. What
was easier, on a dark night, than to lie in wait for the dog-cart, at
a dark turn in the road, aim a stone at whoever was driving—and
if that wasn't effective, something more deadly? Assuming I'm
right, what happened was, he struck de Boulter with a stone, the
dog-cart crashed into a tree, the groom was stunned either with
the fall or by a blow from behind—and then Despenser smashed
de Boulter's head in with a large stone.' Mallett yawned. 'Curious
how evidence is sometimes preserved in a traditional narrative,' he
said. 'Like a fossil in a rock. I noticed, Mrs. Barratt, you repeated
a bit of evidence you must have heard direct from your mother,
just as she must have heard it from those who told the story at the
inquest: namely, that there was no trace of blood on the tree with
which the dog-cart collided, but there was a jagged stone near by,
which might have accounted for the damage.'

He rolled over on his back again. 'So you see,' he said, 'how
it came about that Lindy got everything wrong. She committed

murder—by omission, that is—because Arran omitted to tell her the truth until fifty years later.—I wonder if, now, she'll spare a flower or two for Mary Dazill's grave—eh, Fitzbrown?'

In a few minutes, gentle snoring stirred the newspaper covering Mallett's face. Fitzbrown said violently:

'If she doesn't, I will. They hated Mary Dazill because she was different.'

Mrs. Barratt said mildly: 'I think she must have had a rather difficult character.'

'Ah, well,' said the Vicar, 'it's well to remember—one can't have too much charity.'

'Imagination,' corrected Fitzbrown.

'Loving kindness,' suggested Mrs. Barratt.

'Well, gentlemen'—the Vicar looked at his watch—'it's four o'clock. You'll stay the rest of the night, and to breakfast?'

5

It was half-past seven next morning. A pleasant smell of bacon floated upstairs. A telephone-bell rang. Fitzbrown, forgetting where he was, sat up suddenly in bed, tousle-haired and red-eyed. Recollecting, he lay back again with a sigh.

A minute later, there was a tap on his door. The Vicar entered without waiting for permission.

'It's Miss de Boulter's chauffeur on the 'phone,' he said. 'Fitzbrown, will you come at once? I'm afraid there's been more trouble. I've called Mallett already. They found her lying on the bed beside her sister—and they're afraid—'

Fitzbrown nodded slowly. 'Poison?'

The Vicar gaped. 'Yes. How did you know?'

'There was a bottle of digitalis on the bedside table,' he said. 'Enough to kill three persons. Her sister's medicine, of course. It was full.'

The Vicar came forward a step. 'You should have removed it.'

'Should I?' said Fitzbrown.

THE END